THE RELUCTANT

HOLLYWOOD

P.I.

THE RELUCTANT

HOLLYWOOD

P.I.

An anthology of
twelve short stories
by
William Karl Thomas

MEDIA MAESTRO - BOOK DIVISION

Cover photo and design by William Karl Thomas
Copyright © 2022 by William Karl Thomas

ISBN 978-1-62768-028-8

Printed in the United States of America

This book is a work of historical fiction within which many real persons and/or events have been described. However, all of the dialogue, all of the non-historical persons, and many of the events, are a product of the author's imagination, making any resemblance of such characters to real people purely coincidental.

Published May 2022

MEDIA MAESTRO - BOOK DIVISION
P.O. Box 50672, Tucson AZ 85703
(520) 303-7805
info@mediamaestro.net
www.mediamaestro.net/books.htm

CONTENTS

SNAKE IN THE GRASS

I never met any private investigator who said to himself, "Oh, this sounds like a great profession, I think I'll become a Private Investigator like Sam Spade." Every P.I. I met was either a Police Academy drop-out, an ex-con, or, like myself, someone desperate to find a part time job while they pursued something better in life.

Of course, in our early teens we saw classified ads in the backs of comic books and the men's magazines our fathers and older brothers hid under their mattresses. These ads claimed, "Become a Private Investigator in one week. Complete course and investigative kit only $25." The boy across the street from me was two years older and earned more money than me, and showed me the "kit" which included a tin badge that said "Graduate of S.O.P.I, School of Private Investigation." The rest of the kit had a letter size diploma that said the same thing, an eight page pamphlet that constituted the entire 'course,' and a 'fingerprint kit' consisting of an ink pad, a pill bottle filled with carbon powder, Scotch tape, and printed forms to apply the 'prints.' When I suggested the diploma should not say S.O.P.I, but instead read S.U.C.K.E.R., he didn't talk to me for two weeks.

In the late 1950's, the something better in my life was to attempt to make movies with my talented friends, with me as a collaborative screenwriter and a cinematographer. But, fresh out of the service and trying to shake off the horrors of the Korean War, I was just another kid in my middle twenties trying to 'make it' in Hollywood. To save money, I shared a rear cottage with an aging guitarist named Murphy, Murph for short. Unable to make a living as a guitarist, he held a part time job as a security guard guarding the homes of Hollywood's more affluent residents. The company he worked for was owned by an ex-F.B.I. agent named Mark Angel, and included private investigative services.

Because I had enough knowledge of audio electronics to work with motion picture sound equipment, Murph informed me that Mark Angel was interested in a new technology involving 'wireless microphones' which, in those days, sold for the humongous price of fifty dollars each. I found a circuit in one of the latest electronic magazines, invested a few bucks in parts, and used an ice cube tray to build twelve epoxy filled ice cube size wireless mike modules with wires sticking out for the microphone, battery, and antennae. I got Murph to secretly plant one in Mark's office, recorded Mark's private conversation with his second in command from a location across the street, then played the recording for him minutes later as my sales pitch to sell him my 'bugs,' as he called them. But Mark's second in command didn't know how to use the mikes, so Mark hired me for the then considerable salary of five dollars an hour to install them.

My first assignment was to install bugs in the living room and master bedroom of Donald O'Connor's house just North of Franklin Avenue. O'Connor worked in Las Vegas a lot, and his new young wife remained in Hollywood where she entertained a lot. I will not speculate why he wanted recorded surveillance of his home, but he had provided us with a key. I waited until the house was obviously vacant, went in and succeeded in installing the bugs, but heard people entering the front door before I could leave. I retreated into the patio and hid in a poolside garden shed as a number of people began to party inside and start to migrate to the patio. There was a downhill slope covered with ivy behind the house, and a stairway consisting of two foot diameter sections of a redwood tree used as stepping stones down to a chain link perimeter fence.

As I started down the stepping stones, I heard a familiar sound from my childhood in the Gulf Coast swamps, the chilling sound of a rattlesnake's rattle. And there he was, barely seen by the light of the setting sun, all three feet of him coiled on a stepping stone halfway to my fence goal. I instinctively reached for the .380 MAB hammerless automatic pistol in the shoulder holster under my coat, for which I had a P.I. license, but didn't retrieve it as the sound would have attracted the party goers. I considered going around him, but feared what unknown members of his family might be hidden in the ivy. He hissed at me, and I hissed back. "Go away, you fucking idiot. Don't you know I used to kill you guys just to sell your rattles and skins to the tourists?" But he either didn't believe me, or realized he had the advantage with more and more house guests moving onto the patio.

I surreptitiously retreated to the garden shack, found a bumper jack, and sneaked back to my rendevous with that stubborn rattlesnake. He continued to hiss at me, to which I replied, "Unfortunately for you, my friend, I am not a Buddhist," and whacked his head flatter than a pancake.

It was a challenge getting over the spurs at the top of the chain link fence, and walk a very long circuitous route to get back to my car parked across the street from the house. I dutifully recorded six more hours of the party inside before all was silent and I gave up and went home.

The next day I set the two reels of recorded tape on Mark's desk, then upended a gunny sack as the dead rattlesnake plopped on his desk and he rapidly backed his chair three feet, crashing into the wall. He glared angrily at me and shouted, "What the hell!"

I told him I would no longer work for him solo, that I required at least one assistant as a lookout and/or bodyguard. I also asked for a raise, but didn't get it, probably because he was pissed at me dropping the snake on his desk. But he did agree to provide a second man on future installations.

I don't think he trusted me, fearing I might bug his office again as I did in my audition. He made me provide him with anti-bugging detectors and teach his secretary how to sweep his office, which I'm sure he made her do after every visit I made there. Thereafter he gave me the nickname 'Snake' or 'Snake in the Grass.'

THE END

WILEY COYOTE

Mark Angel had only two other P.I.s when I started working for him. John was the 'bad boy' who, despite his long legs and pot belly and balding red hair, was very adept at physical intimidation and, when needed, violence. The other guy, Tracey, while physically endowed with height and strong shoulders and a good physique, was a 'pretty boy,' and he knew it. He was obsessed with how many aging female stars and up and coming starlets with whom he'd scored, but his inventory of conquests would reach a limit and he wasn't aware that he was repeating the same stories from previous hours.

Tracey knew nothing of electronics, but he loved the latest gadgets. He was the first person I knew to have a car phone, and he would proudly display the two foot square box of tube electronics in his trunk that operated it.

True to his word, Mark sent the two of us out together on my second assignment. The location was on a tertiary road of Mullholland Drive, named after the engineer who, designed The Los Angeles Aqueduct, a series of dams that sucked all of Northern California's water away from the farmers to feed Southern California's real estate expansion. When one of the dams failed and killed thousands of people, Mullholland was removed from the project and died of a stroke. The intrigue of that bit of political financial chicanery was told, in a rather veiled murky fashion, in Roman Polanski's movie, *Chinatown*.

By the time Tracey and I were working on this road that ran along the top of the Hollywood Hills, it was best known for all its little hilltop cul de sacs where the rich and famous lived. A few of the undeveloped cul de sacs offered spectacular views of the glittering lights of Hollywood, while the celebrated occupants of cars parked there steamed up their windows while they increased the population of tinseltown.

This time I had been assigned for my photographic expertise, rather than my bugging skills. We were parked on a hill where we could view the subject's backyard on another hill. We played tag team, and usually it was Tracey who had the better car and would tail the wife if she left the house, while I'd remain to see who might come and go in her absence.

My little Volkswagen Karman Ghia had no car phone, but I had designed a camera mount that attached to the car door and, when the car was at right angles to the house on the adjoining hill, I could maneuver my Exacta camera and 400mm telephoto lens to look into any part of the back yard and through the expansive patio windows and glass doors into half of the house interior.

But the most memorable thing about this assignment was not the wife, who showed no signs of her suspected infidelity during two weeks of surveillance, but, rather, the family dog, a beautiful St. Bernard who, poor thing, was kept in the back yard on a long chain attached to a large oak tree. Our shotgun mike listening device overheard conversations that revealed it was easier to chain the dog than repair the extensive amount of fencing around the several acres of grounds.

There was a third hill facing the hill with the house and the hill with our cars. On the side of that hill there protruded a concrete drain pipe about three feet in diameter. On the second night I was there, I saw a coyote walk from the interior of the pipe to its opening, then lay in wait as it stared at the St. Bernard, who didn't seem to notice the coyote from two hundred feet away. The wife brought out a large bowl filled with dog food and placed it about twenty feet from the tree, slightly less than the length of the St. Bernard's chain, then she re-entered the house as the dog began to eat.

The scraggly looking coyote leisurely walked over to within sight of the dog, who began barking, then the coyote retreated out of sight as the wife came out to investigate. When the wife left, the coyote casually presented himself again to the dog, who barked again, and the coyote retreated again, and the wife inspected and left again. The third time the coyote presented himself, the wife did not come out to inspect. The coyote leisurely walked around the tree in circles just out of reach from the dog who, barking loudly, followed him in circles around the tree until his chain was so short he could no longer reach the food.

The coyote leisurely ate the dogs' food, viewed the barking dog with a look of disdain or possibly compassion, then retreated back into the drainpipe.

I only worked twelve hour night shifts on this assignment, and saw the coyote pull his trick on the dog every single night I was there. I regretted when Tracey got tired of tailing the wife's shopping trips and I had to follow her, asking Tracey when I returned if the coyote had appeared, but Tracey wasn't interested, spending most of his time on his car phone talking to potential new romantic conquests.

I remembered a French children's poem, Maitre Corbeau et Maitre Renard, about the fox who conned the crow out of the piece of cheese he had by flattering the crow for his singing voice, getting the crow to sing and drop the piece of cheese, which the fox snatched. While I could not exactly translate the St. Bernard's barking, and while the coyote never made a sound, and while the fox and the coyote's techniques were different, I had to admire that scraggly wild canine's instincts and reasoning. Certainly we humans admire the big beautiful St. Bernard's appearance far more than that lean ill kept coyote with his hair matted in all directions by his squirming through a filthy drain pipe. Certainly we might never be able to trust that wild wiley coyote were we to invite him into our homes. But he taught me something about how to deceive your enemies and beware of in others. With patience and cunning, you can lead your competition to limit their access to the prize you seek.

THE END

ELVIS' EGGS

One of mobster Mickey Cohen's nightclubs near Fairfax and Santa Monica Boulevards was called The Near and Far. The strippers who worked there preferred to be called ecstadesiasts, which means erotic dancers. The most attractive and popular ones were well paid and made even more off the commissions on drinks bought for them, plus tips from admirers who they may or may not have favored with their charms. Occasionally, one of the girls would acquire an admirer who turned into a stalker, or even into a psycho who would aggressively demand attention or commitment from her.

Because I was Mark Angel's go-to man for anything related to show business, and possibly because John Madden would be too crude and Tracy would be too sexually predatory, I was hired by the management as a temporary bodyguard to a dancer who had acquired a stalker. The job was actually two-fold, to protect the dancer and to try to spot the stalker among the club's audience of primarily horny men. The dancer's stage name was Venus and she had received phone calls, letters, and notes left in the club telling her to pack some warm clothes preparatory to being kidnaped and taken to a Northern climate. He didn't use the word kidnaped, but rather "so you can be swept off your feet and carried to my ice palace where you will experience the greatest sexual delights of your life." Some of the other dancers wanted to volunteer to be his victim.

Venus did not like the idea of having a bodyguard, the main reason being that, though she was married to a successful music arranger who worked for several major television shows, she lived a sexually liberal lifestyle which she claimed was a mutual agreement with her husband. Of the six dancers in the show, two had husbands or boyfriends who were in prison, two were lesbians who lived together, one was unattached, and Venus was the only one with a successful career and, according to her, a successful marriage. The two with partners in prison came on to me once I started the gig, and Venus did also, but I always shied away from marriage triangles. Unfortunately for me, the only one I was attracted to and comfortable with was the unattached girl named Bambi, a very petite innocent looking brunette who appeared almost too young to be working in a bar.

My job was to escort Venus from her home to the club, try to see if I could spot the stalker in the club during the seven hours it was open, and escort Venus back to her home. When she left the club, sometimes Venus wanted to go someplace else, and I was obliged to extend my hours to include those sorties, which sometimes included hours sitting outside the door of some unknown man's residence, but I usually ended each night between three and six in the morning. Mark Angel didn't pay overtime, but, in a day when most clerical workers made two dollars or less an hour, the five dollars an hour Mark paid was worth taking a few risks and about the same as most cops made.

Venus was a little concerned about the stalker, because we all knew all it took was a bottle of chloroform and a getaway car, and a few such victims had died of an unintended overdose of chloroform from a bumbling kidnapper. But she pretended to be unconcerned and insisted my hours at the club be spent running errands for her like picking up her cleaning at an all night dry cleaning establishment, and getting her and all the girls takeout food from Cantor's delicatessen on Fairfax. Even though the girls were on-stage from ten to fifteen minutes at a time, they were trapped in the club drinking with the customers almost seven hours a night. Sometime between ten and twelve in the evening I made a food run to Cantors.

When we ate our food in the communal dressing room behind the stage, I always tried to sit with Bambi and get to know her. "So, Bambi, is this your entry level into show business, maybe films eventually?"

She almost choked on her corned beef sandwich. "Oh, hell no. I didn't just fall off a turnip truck. I'm going to U.S.C. to get a degree in psychology. That's where the surefire money is, not show business."

I was duly impressed. "So, this is how you're putting yourself through college?"

She picked a piece of fatty corned beef out of her teeth. "Actually, my parents are putting me through college. This job is twofold. I'm going to use the experience as research for an eventual Doctoral Dissertation on on the male libido. And the extra bucks will provide me more pocket money than my parents are willing to provide."

I held up a paper plate for her to drop the corned beef fat. "Then maybe you'd like to have dinner with me. You could interview me for your dissertation. I could be a control figure, like a member of the staff who was not motivated to be there because of prurient interest."

She frowned. "Prurient interest?"

I set the paper plate down on her makeup table. "A legal term meaning 'sexual' interest."

She got up as she heard the comedian onstage start her introduction. "I never knew a man..... or a dinner invitation.....that didn't involve 'prurient' interest."

That was the night that Jimmy John showd up in blue jeans, cowboy boots, cowboy hat, cowboy embroidered shirt, and a bolero neckpiece with a sterling silver mounted turqoise that matched his huge belt buckle. I was backstage to carry Venus' makeup kit and clothes bag when the owner ushered him in, saying, "This is your lucky night, ladies. Jimmy John here has come to invite you to a party up at Elvis Presley's house. He's Evis' head roadie."

Jimmy John was two thirds the owner's height and half his weight, and his very large mouth was stretched into a perpetual grim. "That's right ladies. My boss, Elvis, heard about your headliner, Venus, and wants to meet her. But there's lots of important people up there who all you ladies might like to meet, not to mention lots of food and booze!"

While all the other girls showed interest, Venus looked aloof as she said coldly, "No way, roadie. Tell Mr. Swivel Hips Venus is going home to her husband." She trailed her finger across my chin as she swept past me on her way to the back door. "Com'on, Max."

Jimmy John looked upset. "But....Ma'm....Elvis is counting on me!" He turned and looked desperately at the other girls. "But, you girls, you'll come, wont 'cha?"

The two lesbians followed Venus without speaking. The two girls with husbands in prison nodded eagerly. And Bambi smiled and said, "Hell yes, I'll go."

I whispered in Bambi's ear. "You realize this is not some cocktail party with tuxedos and evening gowns. This is probably a cowboy barbecue at which Jimmy John here is as good as it gets."

She raised one eyebrow. "No. Elvis is as good as it gets."

I raised an eyebrow. "I never took you for a groupie."

She shrugged. "Research. Remember?"

Venus opened the back door and yelled angrily. "Max! I'm waiting!."

Bambi chuckled. "Go, bodyguard. Earn your keep."

Like many nights during that two weeks, Venus made me take her to an apartment hotel on Sunset Boulevard instead of her home. I sat in the lobby until sunrise, and the generous nightclek shared his coffee pot with me, telling me stories about the aged movie stars who lived there, and their complaints about their fall from leading film roles to supporting television roles. When, at last, I delivered Venus to her front door, I had barely returned to my car when she came out her front door again and called to me. "Max, Bambi wants you to pick her up. She's at a phone booth at Miller's Drive and Sunset Strip with no cab fare. Can do? She's still on the line."

I yelled back. "Tell her I'll be there in fifteen...twenty minutes."

As Venus shut her door and I slammed my car door, a male neighbor yelled angrily out his window, "Shut the hell up!"

I pulled up to the phone booth and Bambi opened the door, but didn't get it. "Before I get in this car, promise me you wont say 'I told you so,' or try to lecture me."

I raised both eyebrows. "Only if you tell me what happened that left you stranded in a phone booth."

She hesitated, then got in. "Okay, but not until I have something to eat. I haven't eaten since that corned beef sandwich last night."

I couldn't hide the sarcasm in my voice. "What, no barbecue?"

She sounded exasperated. "Yes! They had barbecue, flown in from Kansas City, but it was too spicy hot to eat."

I tried not to sound too eager. "I could fix you breakfast at my place. I make a fabulous Denver omelet."

She looked at me sadly. "Don't take this personally, maybe some other time, but I've had enough sex for tonight. Can't we go somewhere that's open at this hour?

I suppressed my disappointment. "Cantor's is open twety four hours."

She smiled weakly. "Oh, yeah, I like blintzes."

I chose a booth at the rear of Cantor's main room so our conversation would not be heard. She ordered her blintzes and I ordered two soft boiled eggs. When the waitress left, I said, "Soooooo!"

She sighed deeply. "Yes, it was a bunch of cowboy roadies and Jimmy John was the cream of the crop, just like you said."

I softened my sarcasm. "I thought Elvis was as good as it gets."

She brightened. "Yes, he was. And he thought I was the cream of the crop, and we spent the night together."

I tried to sound nonchalant. "And is that when you became sated with sex?"

She bit her lip, then said, "Let's just say I never reveal my research. You'll have to read my dissertation."

The waitress set our coffees down. "You may have some legal problems with that dissertation, particularly if you attend a Southern college."

She shook her head. "Oh, I would never name names. That would be unethical."

I put sugar and cream in my coffee. "So, how did you end up down at that phone booth?"

She shrugged. "We started to eat breakfast and something happened that upset Elvis, so he had Jimmy John come take me from his apartment and told him to drive me home. But Jimmy John tried to take me to his room and, when I refused, he drove me only as far as the gate and left me there. I had to walk down to Sunset Strip."

The waitress set our food down and, as Bambi started to put jelly on her blintzes, I cut the top of my eggs off

14

with a knife and scooped the whole egg into the bowel without breaking the yolk. I asked, "What happened that upset Elvis?"

She looked up from her blintzes and said, "I don't know if I should tell you."

I salted my egs, then picked one whole unbroken egg up with my spoon, put it in my mouth, closed my eyes and smiled as the yolk broke and flooded my mouth with its warm rich taste. When I opened my eyes, Bambi was staring at me with a surprised expression and said, "That's it!"

I said, "What's it?" Then I picked up the second egg, put it in my mouth, closed my eyes, and smiled as the second yolk flooded my taste buds.

When I opened my eyes again, Bambi was pointing at my plate with an even greater surprised expression on her face. "That's it! That's what happened! You eat your eggs just like Elvis eats his!"

I was puzzled. "It may be peculiar moreso to Southerners, but I'm sure many people in many cultures eat their eggs that way. So, why would that upset him? "

She slumped down against the pink Naugahyde backrest of the booth. "Because I commented that he had the same expression on his face when he squished the eggs in his mouth that he had when he had an orgasm in bed."

I shrugged. "Well, I can believe that, but I still don't see why that observation would upset him."

She sighed. "I upset him when I told him I'm a psych major and I suspected the pleasure he got from the egg breaking in his mouth was probably related to his infancy and nursing at his mother's breast." She sat up and started cutting her blintzes. "He accused me of saying he was an infant and that he had some incestuous fixation on his mother when he had orgasms." She shook her head as she speared a section of blintz. "I mean, after all the praises he had heaped on me just hours before, I couldn't....I can't understand why he would misinterpret my innocent observation."

I sipped my coffee. "I can't speak for Elvis or whatever insecurities he might have about his masculinity, but I can give you a word of advice."

She smiled sarcastically. "Okay. Share with me the wisdom of a stripper's bodyguard."

I tried not to look judgmental. "I don't know if psychologists have to take the Hippocratic Oath, but the phrase 'do no harm' applies to many things, including sexual encounters. Keep in mind that in sex, everyone is vulnerable, and each party is seeking affirmation. Find something about the encounter to praise your partner with. Save your clinical observations for your dissertation. And if you ever have one of my Denver omelettes, don't tell me that the mushroom, green onions, tomatoes, and cheddar cheese remind you of your menstrual flow."

She frowned. "Oh God. Now you've ruined your Denver omelette for me forever. Do you make any other breakfast specialities?"

My heart beat a little faster. "How about eggs Benedict?"

Her eyes widened. "Ohhhhhh! I love eggs Benedict. How about, the night after you take that bitch Venus home for the last time, you pick me up at closing and make me some eggs Benedict?"

I raised my coffee cup in toast. "Here's to successful research."

She smiled as she clinked her cup against mine. "And the wisdom of a stripper's bodyguard."

THE END

COSMO ALLEY

Cosmo Street is not an ally, but a street, even if it is only one block long. It is paved and has sidewalks, and even a few lamposts with lights. True, back in the 1950's, it had no storefronts, only the backs of buildings like the Hollywood Library and the Ivar Theater, so it kinda looked like and served the purpose of an alley. You'd think that, running between Hollywood Boulevard and Selma Avenue and being only two blocks from the famous intersection of Hollywood and Vine, people would be more familiar with it, but it was practically unknown before Herbie Cohen and Bennie Shapiro opened the Cosmo Alley Coffee House cum nightclub in 1957.

Herbie Cohen was a nephew of mobster Mickey Cohen. When Mickey Cohen wore out his welcome in New York and moved to California, he concentrated on owning nightclubs which were prime venues for the types of vices he provided. Herbie, however, was young enough to catch the 'show biz' bug, and ultimately became a manager of such talents as Linda Ronstadt, Odetta, and Mark Zappa. At the beginning of his West Coast career, he opened successful coffeehouses such as The Unicorn on Sunset Strip, and Cosmo Alley.

He installed his friend, Benny Shapiro, as manager and minority co-owner of these establishments so Herbie could concentrate on being a talent manager and impresario. But differences between them arose, and Benny was eventually squeezed out of both enterprises, only to establish his own successful beatnik night club, The Renaissance, in an old house on Sunset Strip directly across from famous Ciro's Nightclub.

Benny was replaced in Cosmo Alley with a salaried manager, Jack Sikking, who had turned a failing old Nightclub on Sunset Boulevard into a wildly successful new entity he renamed The Purple Onion. His wild decor and 'partly gay, partly beatnik, partly West Coast jazz' policy had catapulted The Purple Onion to the top of the 'In' people's list. He began to work the same magic on Cosmo Alley, painting the walls black, then painting the exposed overhead plumbing gold and silver, and, where the plaster was damaged on the walls, he further exposed the underlying brick and sanded it bright red. He hired beautiful girls as waitresses, some the wives of famous jazz musicians, and costumed them in skin tight leotard bottoms and custom made Robin Hood style pointed toe shoes, elfin hats and fringed short coats just short enough to expose their shapely derrieres.

At the Purple Onion, the original owners had handled the cash flow system while Jack had concentrated on everything else. At Cosmo Alley, Jack had to handle the cash flow and thought he was safe because he put his boyfriend in charge of the cash register. However, he discovered a great disparity between the headcount coming through the door and the register tally at the end of the night. Not knowing who to suspect, he turned to Mark Angel to plant a spy among the staff who might see or hear about any hanky panky. As the only person on Mark's staff who knew about nightclubs or was young enough to pass for a beatnik, I was given the assignment to pose as a bartender and sniff out the culprit.

It did not take me more than two nights to realize there was no one culprit, but Jack's entire chorus line of multi-ethnic sex symbol waitresses who exploited the fact that Jack was using stock customer receipt pads which the waitresses could purchase duplicates of in any stationary store. They simply wrote every other receipt on a pad they had purchased and pocketed the cash collected for those receipts. Jack thought that handing out pads to the waitresses at the beginning of the night and keeping a tally of which pad numbers were assigned to which girls was sufficient. I stayed up all night the second night in order to phone Mark Angel in the morning and tell him I could make a report. As usual, he berated me for being so naive and told me to say nothing for at least two, preferably three weeks before filing a report, as a two day assignment wasn't worth processing through his office. I had grown used to his lecture and resigned to letting the case ride the whole three weeks.

The three weeks were eventful. They began with an appearance by Theo Bikel, who had bought a 25% ownership of the club, headlining a week of Russian and Yiddish folk music, accompanying himself on the balalaika. Already established on Broadway for his starring role in *Fiddler on the Roof*, he had followed that up with three notable film roles in 1951 for *The African Queen*, in 1952 for *Moulin Rouge*, and in 1957 for *The Enemy Below*. Only 33 at the time, his bearded face and heavy build enabled him to play older roles, even if his abdomen and his balalaika were difficult to negotiate through the narrow door of his closet sized dressing room at Cosmo Alley. He had a beautiful young blonde groupie who was enthralled by her "big Russian bear," and delighted when he taught her how to drink champagne and traditionally smash the stemmed glass against the stone wall in the club's patio. Jack was in his late twenties, only a few years older than me, and, when I joined him in the patio to watch the spectacle of the blonde beauty and the Russian bear, he turned to me with a frown and said,

"Doesn't he know those damn glasses cost us a buck a piece?"

I had talked to the young blonde earlier, and I said to Jack, "I would have thought you'd be more concerned about the fact that she's under the legal drinking age, which could affect your license."

Jack's eyes widened in panic. "Oh shit! He owns 25% of the club. How can I tell him she can't even sit in the audience, much less toast him with champagne?"

I shrugged. "Maybe you could remind him that, in California, the drinking age is also the age of consent."

Jack narrowed his eyes at me. "Okay, Mr. Private Investigator, you guys know about all that legal shit, and I thank God you do, but now's when you begin to earn your keep. YOU are going to tell Mr. Russian Bear that his groupie girlfriend has to go, or, at least, stay locked in that closet of a dressing room until closing."

I winced. "I don't think that exactly fits my job description."

Jack rolled his eyes. "I don't know what Mark Angel is paying you, but I know what he's charging me, and I think he'd agree to anything I'd ask you to do rather than have me hand this case over to another agency."

I sighed, then turned and walked over to Bikel. "Excuse me, Mr. Bikel, I have a message for you."

Bikel looked at me for a half a second before turning back to smile blissfully at the blonde. "Yes?"

I looked over at Jack, then back at Bikel. "The management asked me to inform you that your friend is below the legal drinking age and this club could lose its license if her I.D. was checked by a licensing agent."

He turned to look at me with a pained smile. "Well, that's highly unlikely, and I think we can bend the rules a little in this case."

I inhaled deeply. "They also wanted me to inform you, in case you weren't familiar with California law, that the drinking age is the same as the age of consent."

Bikel was not smiling and his eyes narrowed as he turned to stare at me with a menacing look. He looked past me to Jack, who turned away and pretended to be talking to someone else. Then Bikel's menacing stare softened as he looked back at me and asked, "You're the bartender, right?"

He didn't know I was an investigator. "Right."

Bikel reached in his pocket and pulled out a roll of bills, peeling off three twenties which he handed to me. "I've watched you talking to the staff. I think you can handle this. If you wanna save this liquor license, just go along with me, and I'll take care of the manager." He turned to the blonde. "Sweetheart, come over here." The blonde finished her champagne and smashed the final champagne glass against the wall before joining us. "Baby, remember that movie I was telling you about, *The Defiant Ones*, the next movie I'm going to make?"

Her eyes widened. "Oh, yes, Daddy Bear. You said you'd get me a part, and I'd get to meet Tony Curtis and Sydney Poitier."

Bikel nodded. "Right, well this.....what's your name?"

I must have looked surprised. "Max."

Bikel patted her shoulder and my shoulder simultaneously. "Yeah, Max here is an Associate Producer on that film and he's gonna take you around the corner to The Brown Derby restaurant and buy you dinner while you tell him all about your baton twirling championship and that play you did in highschool. I want the two of you to wait for me there until I'm through here and I join you."

She frowned. "Oh, Daddy Bear, I wanted to hear you play your funny looking Russian guitar."

22

He hugged her and kissed her forehead. "Oh Sweetheart, I promise I'll give you a special private concert back at the hotel, but, for now, go with Max here and wait for me."

She stood on her tiptoes and kissed his lips, then blinked and smiled. "Whatever you want, Daddy Bear."

That wasn't the first or last time I dined at The Brown Derby, or the first or last time I listened to the naive and sometimes pathetic background of a small town beauty queen or contest winner or just plain aggressively ambitious pretty girl who caught the eye of an 'A' or 'B' list celebrity. It was, however, the first and last time Jack Sikking let me leave the premises during working hours

In addition to the elfin waitresses, the Cosmo Alley staff consisted of Jack Sikking's boyfriend who sat at the register all night, a second bartender who was Dave Brubeck;s younger brother, a doorman who was Herbie Cohen's friend and there to keep tabs on how much money should be walking through the door, and two dishwasher's I had hired for Jack who were music students at the Westlake School of Jazz, Paul George and Louis Martinez.

Paul was a clarinetist who looked like Fidel Castro, and the rebellious son of a father who owned the St. George musical instrument company, including Pearl Drums. As Arabs, Paul and his father were anti-Semites, and Paul assumed my tendency to use Yiddish expressions was evidence I was Jewish. So George was confused by my support to help the Westlake students acquire instruments and find jobs, always expecting there to be a 'hook' in my gestures. Eventually George would stop rebelling against his father, take over the St. George musical instrument empire, make Louie Martinez a partner in the company, live in Japan where most of the instruments were manufactured, and get stranded on a desert island for two years in the Pacific when his yacht sank.

But back then he was grateful to wash dishes at Cosmo Alley so he didn't have to appeal to his father for money. He was also happy to help me wrap the frozen steaks and half empty wine bottles we saved and hid in the trash, which we would retrieve after the club closed and we'd go to different waitresses homes to party.

Bikel's appearance was followed by a two week booking of one of Herbie's entertainment management clients, Odetta. On Odetta's closing night, she invited everyone over to her boyfriend Dannys' house on Hoover. It was a modest old house, the kind they used to call 'shotgun houses' because the rooms were all in one line and with all the doors open you could shoot a shotgun through the length of the house without hitting anything. Danny had made a psychedelic pad out of it, murals and mosaics of vibrant colors and bits of colored bottle glass, mirror, and sequins vying with fabric and macrame to carry Daliesque designs from wall to ceiling to floor, from room to room with nothing to stop the flow of color except beaded curtains that alternated beads with polished spoons and forks and keys and miniature speakers that were hooked into the fabulous hi-fi system.

There was every kind of booze. There was a huge water pipe with six pipe sterns to a circle of large multicolored velvet cushions around it, and a king's ransom of Columbian gold marijuana in a beautiful brass tea caddie that matched the hookah water pipe. There was an exquisite menorah with each of its nine candle drip cups holding a goodly supply of bennies, dexies, red dragons, and pills of every color and description. Would you believe, everybody got stoned, except me, of course.

Through the haze that started to give me a contact high, I saw Paul George making out with one of the waitresses, and, just beyond them, Jack Sikking who was glaring daggers at his Nelly cash register friend who was idolizing Danny, who was the very embodiment of the saying 'black is beautiful.' The waitress was praising the abundance of drugs Danny had provided, and started comparing it to the wine and steaks we ripped off at the club. She was obviously headed toward discussing skimming the cash next, and Jack was standing barely four feet from her reclining form. I signaled Paul with a finger across my throat to shut her up, but he was so stoned he just leered at me and returned his attention to her anatomy. The more she talked, the more Jack became tom between an interest in what she was saying and the interest his friend had in Danny. When Jack's attention definitely shifted to the waitress, I crawled over to where she lay entangled with Paul and clamped my mouth over hers in what I hoped looked like sex-crazed lust. Paul rose up on his elbows, frowned at me, and crawled off in indignation that I had intruded upon his new conquest. I looked out the comer of my eye to see Jack glaring suspiciously at me. His eyes were bloodshot and he was a little wobbly, so I hoped he'd forget his suspicions by the next day. I took my mouth off the girl's and said, "At least I didn't do what Danny's doing."

That did the trick. Jack whirled around to see his friend doing more of the doing than Danny, who was trying to make a polite retreat. Jack suddenly became more butch than I'd ever seen him. He steadied his thin impeccably dressed frame, ran both hands through his little bit of corn silk hair, and placed a bony but firm hand on his friend's collar, dragging him out of the house with stern pronouncements about overindulging in chemical vices.

As the girl put an arm around my neck and pulled me down on her so hard our teeth banged painfully, I ceased to worry about Jack's suspicions and began to worry about Paul thinking I had cut him out.

When I made my final report, I gave Jack three different cash systems, beginning with custom printed pads that had the club name on them and carbon copies to give the patron with instructions to drop it in a box at the front exit to enter a drawing for a possible future free visit. The eighty percent of patrons who put the carbon copies in the drawing box at the front exit was enough to frighten the waitresses away from using phony receipt pads. The other trick I taught him was to stain the edge of the pads with a laundry detergent solution that, once dry, was invisible, except under ultra-violet light. That would make any fake receipt withoout the stain identifiable and traceable to a specific waitress.

Jack's compliments to Mark Angle of my performance were so effusive that Mark and John Madden were convinced I had sex with Jack and taunted me with that misconception forever after.

THE END

LET THERE BE LIGHT

In the office, Mark Angel often referred to me as 'Snake' or 'Snake in the grass,' because of my first case when I dumped the rattlesnake on his desk. To clients, he referred to me as his 'techie P.I.' because he mostly used me to collect audio and photographic evidence. Some cases had nothing to do with spying or deductive reasoning, they were pure and simple just to go take a picture or record an interview, and the client could have just hired a photographer or a flunky who could operate a tape rcorder for considerably less money.

When Mark asked me to meet a client in his office for what would probably be a photo assignment, John Madden stopped me outside the office door with a big grin on his face and said, "When you meet this client, whatever you do, don't laugh at his name."

I frowned at him. "What's his name?"

John touched my arm. "Mark will tell you, but remember, don't embarrass yourself by laughing at his name." Then he broke up laughing.

I think John was trying to set me up so I would laugh at the client's name when Mark introduced me. I entered the office to find Mark at his desk with a very short man in a very expensive suit seated in one of the two leather upholstered seats in front of the desk. Mark gestured toward the man and said, "Max, this is Attorney Shimmel Fuchs (he pronounced it 'Fukes') who needs some photographic evidence for a court case. Mr. Fuchs, this is Max, my techie P.I. I told you about."

I shook Fuch's hand as I sat in the other chair and Mark continued. "Mr. Fuchs here has an injury case involving a client who fell in that underground parking lot just North of Graumann's Chinese Theater. He needs,....well, you tell him, Mr. Fuchs."

Fuchs was about forty, five feet tall, had a slight build and thin wavy black hair. He looked at me inquisitively, as if he were looking for something in my face or eyes. He spoke dramatically, as if he were delivering a line in a murder mystery play. "Max, can you photograph light?"

I'm sure I looked puzzled, because I was. "I'm not sure I understand, Sir. Photography is dependent upon light. In fact the word photography is composed of the Greek words for 'light' and 'to draw.' Everything I photograph is a record of the reflection of light from the subject."

He closed and opened his eyes. "Yes, of course. What I mean is, my client fell because of the inadequate lighting in an underground parking lot. I've tried to get the court to transport the jury to the parking lot at night so they can see the stairwell lighting, but our request has been denied, I suspect because of cost factors. Can you photograph that parking lot to illustrate the inadequate lighting?"

I sucked air through my teeth in hesitation. Mark moved closer to his desk and leaned forward. "Of course he can. Max is a great photographer, a real professional, he's sold a lot of his stuff to magazines, and provided photographic evidence for a lot of my cases. He can even take motion pictures if you want."

Fuchs looked at me eagerly. "Is that right, Max. Can you photograph how dim the lightning in that parking lot is?"

I could see Mark glaring at me and slightly nodding his head to indicate I should say"Yes." I smiled at Fuchs and said, "Possibly. I'd have to look at the specific area where your client fell. How soon do you need these pictures?"

Fuchs smiled hopefully at me. "I need them in court tomorrow morning."

I watched Mark frown as he pushed his chair back from the desk and shook his head ever so slightly. I knew he was furious that this was a two day assignment and not a two weeks assignment. I tried to salvage what I could to satisfy Mark. "Well, Sir, that's an almost impossibly tight schedule, but I do have my equipment in my car downstairs, and I could try. It would, however, require working throughout the night, which would involve overtime and what we call gold time, plus photographic expenses and..."

Fuchs looked delighted. "That's fine. Cost is no object, as long as there's a reasonable chance you can show up in court with the pictures."

Mark nodded his head imperceptibly as he moved closer to his desk, obviously relieved that I had padded the bill as much as possible. "Well, if we're in agreement, Mr. Fuchs, you can sign our standard contract the secretary has waiting for you in the outer office. Max, after Mr. Fuchs has singed the contract, accompany him to the parking lot so he can show you where his client fell."

While Fuchs signed the contract, John came in with a grin on his face, pulled me aside, and spoke in a stage whisper. "So, did you laugh when Mark introduced you to Mr. Shimmel Fuck? Shimmel Himmel Fuck. Jews have such fucked up names. You laughed, didn't you." I didn't answer him as Fuchs joined me and we headed to the elevators.

It was early evening when we entered the underground parking lot. I carried my press camera folded up and barely hidden under my coat. As we passed between two cars on our way to reach the corner staircase where his client had fallen, Fuchs noticed one of the cars shaking, stopped, then gasped as he saw a couple copulating in the back seat. I grabbed his sleeve and pulled him along with me. As we passed between more cars on our way, Fuchs screamed and grasped my sleeve upon seeing a young hippee boy with tattos and a purple Mohawk haircut kneeling and fellating a uniformed black sailor with his white pants down to his knees. The pair frowned at us for three seconds before the boy renewed his fellation and the sailor leaned back against the wall with his eyes closed.

At the stairwell, I used the trunks of different cars as a tripod to take time exposures of the dimly lit corner from different angles. When we returned to our respective cars parked next to each other on the street, Fuchs looked shaken. "I never saw anything like that when the client showed me that stairwell during the day."

I put my camera in its case and closed my trunk lid. "At night, Hollywood Boulevard becomes a hedonist's playground. Between La Brea and the freeway, you can find every vice imaginable. I'll process these photos tonight and meet you in court tomorrow."

That night I was so sleepy I left the prints in the dryer and when I woke in the morning they were ruined because the emulsion slid off the paper. I hurriedly made new prints, but didn't have time to dry them, so I arrived in court with damp prints rolled in blotter paper. I suggested to Fuchs questions he might ask me. When he put me on the stand and handed my prints to the judge, the judge frowned as he unrolled the blotter paper. He compared my prints, which made the stairwell look dim, to the defense prints, that made the stairwell look bright, and concluded that one set of prints had to be false.

On cross examination, the defense lawyer mentioned the damp prints disdainfully, saying sarcastically, "Where did you learn photography?"

Although his question was rhetorical, I answered with a lie that I knew would give Fuchs an opportunity to use one of my questions. I said, "I learned photography during my four years of service in the Air Force, Sir." In reality, I had bought a press camera when I was thirteen and had been a professional photographer for twelve years before being in that courtroom.

Fuchs picked up my cue and, on re-examination, asked me where and how long I had attended military photographic school. I told a half-truth by saying, "For eight weeks in Washington, D.C., Sir." Actually, I spent eight weeks at a cartographic drafting school in Washington D.C., another eight weeks at a general drafting shool in Texas, and another eight weeks at an engineering drafting school in Cheyenne, all courtesy of the military.

Then Fuchs asked, "And where did you apply these acquired skills during your military service?' The defense objected, but the judge became interested and allowed it.

I acted as if I were in a military court, and answered honestly insofar as my tour of duty. "For one year in the combat zone of Korea, and for six months in England during the Cold War, Sir."

You could see the look of approval on the faces of the judge and the jury. Fuchs continued with another of my questions. "And how do you explain the discrepancy between your photos and the defense's?"

I looked at the judge and the jury as I answered. "Any competent photographer can manipulate a photograph in the camera or the darkroom to look like either of those sets of photos." I held up my Norwood Director light meter, which was the favorite light meter of many famous cinematographers seen in magazine photo stories with a Norwood Director meter hanging around their necks. "Professional photographers measure light in 'foot candles,' as measured by a professional light meter such as this Norwood Director light meter. Most cities consider the very minimum light for any public space at nighttime to be five foot candles. This meter registered two foot candles in that stairwell. My photos, taken just last night, were printed by me to illustrate exactly what I saw. But photos can lie, so you should see that stairwell for yourself with your own eyes to determine which of those sets of photos tell the truth."

From the smiles on the judges face and the murmuring in the jury box, I knew, and Fuchs knew, and even the defense knew, that we had won. The following night the jury was paid extra to visit the parking lot and ultimately side with Fuchs' client. Fuchs wanted to hire me to work for him full time. He even offered to pay for me to take law classes, but I wanted to be free to work on films with my talented friends. I would have no doubt made more money with Fuchs than with Mark Angel. But money cannot buy the adventures I have had.

THE END

THE MUSIC LOVING VOYEUR

Another case, where the client could have avoided Mark's exorbitant fees by simply hiring a photographer, was delivered to me over the phone when Mark gave me the phone number and address of an upscale hillside home facing the Hollywood Bowl, an amphitheatre in the Hollywood Hills. Mark added, "Gimme a record of your time, the portal to portal time from and to your house, the time at his house, and the time you spend to, from, and in the stores."

I was puzzled. "What stores?"

From his tone of voice, I could imagine the frown on Mark's face. "He needs some equipment installed. He'll tell you all about it. And Max, don't make any judgement calls on this one. Just provide what he asks for, and make sure you record those hours."

The house was high on a hillside about a quarter mile directly opposite the stage of the Hollywood Bowl. Southern California houses have a lot of white inside and outside, and Hollywood Hills houses have patios and upstairs balconies overlooking the view. Eli introduced himself by first name only, but, as he led me through a ;hallway lined with huge photo head shots of famous recording artists, I knew, even before I got a side glance of an office lined with framed gold and platinum records, that he was a music producer. Then hallway connected to a huge living room, the ceiling of which was three stories high with a three story high glass wall facing the patio and it's view of the Hollywood Bowl. We ended up on the humongous cantilevered ground floor patio that hung precariously above all his poorer neighbors. The patio was

33

only partially covered by his second and third story balconies on both side of the glass wall.

Eli stood at the patio railing with a hundred foot drop below, then made a frame with his hands facing Hollywood Boswl. "I want to put one here." Then he turned and pointed to a third story balcony. "And another one up there."

I thought I knew, but I had to ask. "One what, sir?"

He looked surprised. "Didn't Mark Angel tell you? I want you to set up one of those new black and white vidicon tube cameras fitted with a telephoto lens that will fill the frame with the stage of the Hollyood Bowl, and I want its output fed to a video recorder and the largest available monitor on that table over there."

I was right. "That's do-able, sir, but, because this balcony is exposed to the weather, perhaps we should put the camera on a tripod and dolly with wheels, and the video recorder and monitor on a wheeled cart? That way they can be moved indoors at night or during bad weather"

He smiled approval. "Excellent idea. Now let's go upstairs."

He did not choose the elevator we had passed in the front hallway, and the trip up the metal spiral staircase in the living room was enough to keep fifty year old Eli in good shape, and challenge twenty-five year old me. The white bedroom carpet was deep enough to polish your shoes in ten steps, and the open door of the bathroom revealed a Jacuzzi tub and his and her hand basins with gold faucets. The balcony was large enough for a table and two chairs and had a breath taking view, but only a fracton of the size of the ground floor patio. I winced. "It wll be tight to get a camera dolly here, sir, and the video recorder and monitor would have to be inside."

34

He nodded. "Oh yes! They'd be beside the bed. And the camera coould be mounted on this metal railing."

I bit my lip. "It's strong enough, but it's not the best angle to view the stage of the Hollywood Bowl."

He wrinkled his brow. "Oh, this one's not for the bowl. It's for that house down there. The one with the swimming pool."

Suddenly I understood Mark's reference to making a judgement call. I sighed. "I see. Well, that will require a shorter telephoto lens to cover that patio."

He shook his head. "Oh no! I want it long enough to fill the frame with two people." He smiled warmly. "My neighbor down there is a porn flm producer. He shoots a lot of his films on that patio. That chaise lounge there has more cum on it than my satin bed sheets ever had." His eyebrows rose. "Say, maybe we could have two cameras up here; the black and white video camera and a still 35mm camera so I could get some color shots, too."

I nodded my head dutifully. "Can do, but, if you want both video and still cameras operable simultaneously, that will mean two telephoto lenses up here and a third on the patio, plus two vidicon cameras, one 35mm camera, two video recorders, two monitors, a dolly, a cart, and a lot of cables."

He shrugged. "Fine! Whatever it takes, it's worth it." He looked dreamily at the patio pool. "Did you ever see Annette Haven? She's one of his favorite stars. I'd walk over hot coals to get to her."

I was trying to comply with Mark's dictum. "No. I was offered a job shooting porn, but I guess I just wasn't brave enough to commit my name to that industry."

He looked at me in amazement. "Do you realize how much sex you could have as a porn cinematographer. Those girls would be dependent on you to make them look good." He looked back at the pool. "Some female recording artists bribe me with sex, but none of them even come close to being as hot as Annette Haven. At least now I'll be able to watch her have sex with somebody else while Maria gives me head."

I spoke at risk of violating Mark's dictum. "How does Maria feel about that?"

Eli chuckled. "Maria's my housekeeper. She does me when I have no other options." He smiled at me. "And she's very happy with the generous salary I pay her."

I installed everything Eli wanted and he praised me to Mark, even though I spent a fortune at Bob Gamble's and Lloyd's Camera on the equipment and padded my hours more tha usual. I researched Annette Haven and had to agree with Eli, just not enough to deal with shooting porn or the hot coals.

THE END

LUCKY STRIKE

Even in the 1960's, Los Angeles International Airport was one of the largest airports in The United States and in the world, certainly it was the largest in California. So it was a big deal when a flight engineers' strike threatened to cripple the industry. The airport is located South of Los Angeles on the Pacific Coast, and Century Boulevard, a major East West artery, runs right into it.

The flight engineer's Union set up temporary headquarters in a Century Boulevard motel not far from the airport. A collection of affected airlines hired Mark Angels' agency to spy on the Union headquarters, and John Madden, Tracey, and I were assigned to do so twenty-four hours a day in shifts that required two of us at a time to be there. John had bribed the motel desk clerk to convince the guests in the room adjacent to the Union headquarters room that they had to be relocated in order to repair the room, so we could have it.

When I arrived, John told me I had to somehow bug the adjacent room, but it was occupied by Union staff twenty-four hours a day. I told him I had to get into that room in order to see their side of our adjacent wall. He bribed a maid to allow me, wearing a green maids' coat, to push her maids' cart into the room for her and wait while she changed their linen. Once I saw what was and wasn't on the wall, I was prepared to bug it from our side of the adjacent room.

I determined where the two by four studs were, then cut a foot square hole in the sheetrock on our side of the wall. Whenever the maid entered, we'd cover the hole with a framed wall print. I saved the sheeteock square I had

37

removed so I could retrofit it when we were ready to leave. I scraped a small hole recess in the sheetrock on the inside of the Unions' wall with nothing but a pinhole in the paper on their side. I cut a small hole in the bottom of a styrofoam cup, ran a mike cord through it from the inside, filled the cup with cotton, and positioned the half inch diameter mike element in the top of the cup with tape to center it and hold the cotton in place. I then duct taped this assembly to the small hole recess in the sheet rock facing the Unions' room and plugged the mike cord into a reel to reel recorder that could record up to two hours continuously.

Reception was great. Every word was clear as a bell, at least when nobody was flushing a toilet in either room. We were able to record their conversations continuously, but one of us was also required to listen on earphones continuously to determine if there was anything significant to report to Mark Angel, who would then decide whether or not to relay it to the clients. Tracey was very bad at this, sometimes falling asleep, sometimes being caught with his little transistor radio or the phone on one ear and one side of the tape monitor headset on the other as he listened to music or talked to a girlfriend. Johnny gave him the graveyard shift for monitoring because it was the least likely to have significant information.

The strike dragged on for weeks, much to the benefit of my bank account, because we had sixteen paid hours and eight hours off daily. Tracey filled the boredom with a supply of girly magazines which piled up beside the bathroom toilet. All of us read them, but Johnny delighted in pounding on the door and accusing whichever one of us who was there of masturbating. This despite the fact that I arrived for my shift one day to find Tracey sitting in the hall floor outside the room smoking. He said, "Don't go in there!"

We each had a key, and I was concerned that John might be sleeping and the Union room wasn't being monitored, so I went in. John was very aggressively screwing the maid he had bribed, her half clothed body bent over the formica table where we ate. His face was almost as red as his hair, and the middle aged Mexican maid was not smiling. I considered the priorities of my job security and chilvalry, then looked the maid in the eye and asked, "Are you okay, m'am?"

Johnny screamed at me without losing a stroke of his hips, "Get the fuck outt'a here you fucking asshole!" The maid looked like she was in pain, but closed here eyes, then opened them and nodded her head up and down to indicate she was okay. I waited in the hall with Tracey until the maid exited thirty minutes later, avoiding eye contact with us.

When we went in, I noted that the recorder was still running, then asked, "Did you have the speaker monitor on?" We used headphones so no one in the Union room could possibly hear any feedback from the speakers, but I thought he might have used them in this case.

He snarled at me as he lit a cigar. "Shouldn't you be asking me if you still have a job, asshole?"

I inspected the recorder and the earphones were still plugged in, indicating he hadn't been monitoring for probably an hour. I looked at him. "Okay, do I still have a job?"

He continued to frown ferociously. "Only because of your techie talents, asshole. But listen to me, mother fucker, if you ever interrupt me like that again, I'll rearrange that pretty face of yours so no cunt will ever fuck you again."

Tracey looked surprised as he looked at Johnny, then me, and said, "HE has a pretty face? Oh well, I guess relative to you."

John snarled at him. "You too, fucker!"

Tracey shrugged. "Whaaaaaat? I stayed out in the hall like you said."

I asked, "John, did you put a white sticker on the recording tape when you stopped monitoring?"

John savored a long drag on his cigar. "No, but go back about an hour to the last thing you heard and monitor everything since then on the speakers with low volume. I'll plug the earphones into the pre-amp and monitor the room while you do that before I leave."

I sighed. "I don't know what we heard last. I wasn't here."

John plugged the headphones into the pre-amp and turned to Tracey. "Oh yeah. Tracey, you review the past hour of the tape with the speakers at low volume."

Tracey grimaced. "I sit in the hall! He interrupts your fuck session! But I gotta review what you failed to monitor?"

John removed the cigar from his mouth, his eyes bulged as he glared at Tracey, and his voiced raised in anger. "Yeah, mother fucker, do it!"

Fortunately, nothing significant was lost during John's "fuck session."

Not unlike many PI assignments, it was 98% boredom waiting for something significant to happen. We had three critical pieces of information to relay to the clients. The first was the Union considering the addition of some heavyweight lawyers. Our heads up information allowed the airlines to hire those lawyers out from under the Union. The second was a safety equipment issue the Union was going to add to their complaints. Our information allowed the airlines to order the equipment and bribe the suppliers to say it had been back ordered before the strike ever began. Finally, a little over three weeks after the strike began, we were able to report to the clients that, because of pressure from the unpaid union members, the Union leadership was ready to capitulate if the airlines didn't cave within a two day deadline.

I felt ambivalent about half the cases I worked on. At heart, I sided with the union for two reasons, because of safety issues, and because of the responsibility of their work. They were the key link in insuring the lives of tens of thousands of passengers daily. As for the salaries, I was less sympathetic, inasmuch as they made several times what I made. And, in some cases, I faced the same challenges they did; there were times when life and death depended upon me, and there were times when my safety was in jeopardy. I have no doubt, if those Union leaders found out what we were doing in the next room, they would sent a bunch of guys as mean and brutal as John in there to "rearrange our faces."

THE END

OVER THE THRESHOLD

Back in the late 1950's and early 1960's, wireless microphones were rare. The earliest commercial ones were very expensive versions used in film, stage, and television production and so problematical that, in most cases, it was easier to use microphones on a 'fishpole' (boom) or strategically located on the set or stage. For the tiny market of private investigative work where sound fidelity was not that critical, entrepreneurs like myself hand wired them in our kitchens using the newly available transistors and encapsulating them in epoxy filled ice cube trays. Because of their rarity, there were no laws concerning them in the beginning, and the FCC (Federal communications Commission) was more concerned about our using the unused radio and television audio bands for reception, rather than our invading people's privacy. An investigator could hook an inexpensive broadcast band transistor radio receiver to his tape recorder to pickup transmissions from the 'bug' he had planted. Bugs could also be planted in the phone box on the outside of the house, eliminating the need to illegally enter the house to plant it in the phone itself.

That was the my first duty in a case that took me to Santa Barbara, even though Mark Angel wouldn't pay me 'portal to portal,' and the time and gas it took me each day to travel there cut into my profits, not to mention that Mark also didn't pay overtime for eighteen hour days and weekends. But, in those days, eighteen hours at five dollars an hour was pretty good for part time work that left me free to pursue occasional film work.

The case was a roadie who had a feud with his country singer employer, and retaliated by bringing a workman's compensation case claiming the heavy band instruments had ruined his back. His evidence included doctor's testimony that was suspect, as it was from one of Hollywood's 'feelgood' doctors known to provide prescription drugs as 'recreational' drugs to performers. I was supposed to provide audio or photographic evidence that there was nothing wrong with his back. But, after several days of monitoring the phone box tap from across the street, I had no verbal confession from him that he or his doctor had lied.

The bulk of his phone conversations were with his girlfriend, and most of that was his angry complaints against his country singer employer. Having worked with quite a few 'A' list temperamental entertainers and film stars, I thought his complaints were naive. Few employers spend much time praising or appreciating their support crew, and everyone above you IS inclined to take credit for any ideas or innovations you provide. I always found it wisest to keep peace with your credit stealing boss, and wait for the rare opportunity to privately communicate to you bosses boss that YOU are the genius behind all those bright ideas. Then you have to convince your bosses boss that, if he promotes you, HE can then take credit for all you do. I am convinced that I am smarter than the majority of my employers, but I learned early on that, to survive, I had to be an asset, and any overt effort to compete made me a threat to them, and unemployed.

Of course, some of his conversations with his girlfriend were pillow talk. Most of it did not come off as intentional phone sex, but, for a roadie who was an aspiring country western performer himself, some of his conversation vacillated between raunchy and poetic. At the risk of arguments with my publisher, but to make the balance of this story understandable, here's some of a conversation with Travis, the roadie, and Tina, his girlfriend. His voice was a bass-baritone, even if his vocabulary was limited. Her voice was like little girl's voice, full of innocence despite her many sexual references. I couldn't help that I began to like them.

****

Travis: "Hey, sweet cheeks, what are you wearing?"

Tina: "Just some old jeans and one of your shirts. I like to wear your shirts because they smell like you."

Travis: "Then why, when you pick me up at work, you bitch that I stink and make me shower before I can hug you?"

Tina: "Well, you DO stink. And, worst of all, when you throw your stinky clothes in the corner and they sour, it's horrible!"

Travis: "How can you love me if you think my sweat stinks?"

Tina: "Your sweat doesn't stink, just when it's been sitting around long enough to sour. When you're on top of me and the sweat runs off your neck and shoulders onto my face and mouth, it tastes salty and smells exciting. I know you don't like me to talk about being with other men, but different men smell differently, and you smell good to me, exciting. So, when I take your sweaty shirt off and put it on a hanger and it dries out for a day or two, then, when I wear it, it has a feint odor of you that I like, and it makes me feel like we're together."

Travis: "I think I understand. It's like how you taste to me when I go down on you. When I was a kid, I never dreamed I'd enjoy reaming a girl's crotch from her clit to her tail bone. God! I can taste you in my mouth right now just thinking of it!"

Tina: "Stop it! Now you're making me believe I can taste your cum in my mouth right now. Why is it you always want me to swallow it?"

Travis: "Wow! 'Cause that's the ultimate acceptance. I mean, that, and when you let me butt fuck you. When you told me you had never done those two things with anybody else, that's when I knew I was in love."

Tina: (Hesitates.) "Wow, Travis, I'm not sure if I should be flattered by that. Your greatest appreciation of me is 'cause I take your cum down my throat and up my butt?"

Travis: "Oh, no, no, no, Baby! I love you for so many reasons. Remember that song I wrote about all the things I love about you."

Tina: "Yeah, as I recall, it cataloged everything you found attractive about my body."

Travis: "No, no! I talked about your voice, it was like a bird call, and the smell of your hair, and, most of all, the way you pronounce my name in the dark. Baby, you gotta know I love you. You're still coming this weekend, aren't you? That's why I got this damn place!"

Tina: "I thought you got it so you'd be closer to your boss and your work."

Travis: "Well, that too, but I got a place that was big enough for the two of us, and nice enough to make you happy. I love you baby, your killer body, your squeaky voice, and all the crazy little things about your personality that make you the hottest chick I've ever known."

Tina: (Hesitates.) "Shut up, Travis. I love you, too. I'll see you this weekend."

****

In anticipation of possibly getting photos of his hauling a humongous trunk on his back while unloading her car, I set up a 16mm movie camera with a huge 300mm telephoto lens which, from three hundred feet away, would fill the frame with a full figure image. I had made a special steel rig to mount cameras in my little Karmen Ghia, and I had the windows heavily tinted to hide the equipment from passer-bys. I also had a long telephoto lens on a 35mm single lens reflex still camera which I could hand hold beside the movie camera, both lenses resting on the top of the partially opened window glass. I had barely gotten everything set up when Tina arrived at ten in the morning. I waited until he came out to the car, she exited, and they embraced. When they broke the embrace, I started the electric drive on the movie camera, hoping his next step would be to remove her luggage and, with any luck, it would heavy enough to put on his shoulder.

But, despite his bending down to retrieve her purse from the car seat and hand it to her, the two just stood there talking. The electric drive on the movie camera could run continuously, but the role of film in the movie camera would only last a few seconds over three minutes. I readied the still camera in case the movie camera ran out of film. Changing film in the movie camera would probably risk missing the needed action. I began to sweat with fear that a weeks work would result in nothing. As the sweat ran off my forehead onto my still camera, I wondered if Tina would think my sweat stank. I began to compose a false report for Mark Angel in my head, void of the reality that I missed filming Travis with a heavy trunk on his back while I was reloading the movie camera. The whirring sound of the movie camera became deafening in my ears, but I dared not turn it off to conserve film and possibly miss the shot. As much as I had grown to like the couple, I was getting mad at them for standing jabbering while my movie film was about to run out.

Finally the unexpected happened. There was no luggage. There was no trunk. But the deliriously happy Travis picked up the deliriously happy Tina and, carrying her in his arms as if she were a feather, he walked fifteen feet to the door, kicked it open without any trace of pain or loss of balance, and, after kissing her passionately on the mouth, carried her into the house and kicked the door shut. Immediately after the door shut, I heard the flick flick flick of the tail end of the movie film run through the camera.

I picked up the film from Pathe Labs, reviewed it in the projector at my studio, and verified that I had the evidence the Workman's Comp lawyers needed. As I sat typing my report for Mark that night, I remembered when I was reviewing aerial photos in Korea with a stereoscopic viewer. Back then I was looking for evidence of airplanes or trucks or tanks or North Korean military personnel on the ground. I remember thinking that if I saw them in the photos, they would probably be annihilated the next day, and they were humans who just wanted to go home just like I did. I felt like I held their lives in my hand, and, for a fleeting second, I thought about sparing those lives. Just then, a siren sounded and seconds later some fifty caliber slugs tore through the tent as we all hit the deck. I heard screams in the adjoining darkroom tent where the aerial films were developed, and I ran over to help pull out the corpses of two of my friends. Then I returned to my desk eager to find and report the planes and the men who may have just taken the lives of my friends.

But Tina and Travis were just two kids who loved each other. I did not hear their conversation in front of the house, but I imagined that the words "the happiest day of my life" might have passed their lips. Because of me, they would see the romantic gesture of him carrying her over the threshold of their first home together on a flickering screen in a courtroom, and he would be fined and possibly do time for fraud. I did not cry when I filed my report of aerial photos in Korea, but I did shed a tear when I reread my report to Mark Angel, and, once again, I felt a reluctance to be a Hollywood P.I..

THE END

SLEEPY LAGOON

I sat in front of Frank Angel's desk. "What've you Got for me?"

Frank picked up a letter and started reading. "Minnesota Mining and Manufacturing Company believes a major Los Angeles electronics store is selling boxed 10 ½" reels of premium 1/4" recording tape that came from a truck shipment that was hi-jacked three months ago. The store is selling it as degaussed used tape, but one of their salesmen bought a roll, sent it to their lab in Minnesota, and they claim it is brand new tape that's never been used." He put down the letter and frowned at me. "They named that store you get all your techie shit from, that one on Olympic Boulevard just West of Vermont. You know anyone on staff there/"

I shook my head. "Not personally."

He picked up a folded section of the Los Angeles Times classified ad section. "In addition to being a parts retailer, they manufacture of line of electronic gear. I called to see if they're hiring sales staff, and they weren't, but they have a new product they're manufacturing and hiring commissioned salesmen to pitch it." He threw the folded page into my lap. "See if you can get hired to sell that krap, you'll be paid the usual only during the hours you're actually working for them. But I want to see copies of your time card, or some verification of those hours."

I frowned. 'What about travel time and expenses?"

He looked at paper work on his desk and waved his hand at me. "There is none. It's not like when I sent you to Santa Barbara or La Jolla. It's local, and I'm not buying you a salesman's business suit. Besides, maybe you'll sell some and get commissions, and maybe you'll get an employee discount on the parts for all the bugs you make for me." He looked up and waved his hand at me again. "Get out of here and don't call me until you can tell me they've hired you."

The store in question was a gigantic electronic supply store with the most competitive prices in town. They did manufacture a small line of hi-fi and professional amplifiers and test instruments. Their new product claimed to be a 'Sleep Machine,' but was simply a white noise generator in a fancy housing that included a low power amp and speaker sufficient to placed on a night stand beside a bed. Limited clinical studies had concluded that white noise could induce sleep in some people. I had built one for Frank, along with a bug sweeper, in order to mask private conversations from any bug. That was one of his initial requirements in hiring me to insure I would never bug his office again.

After a brief interview, the store hired me. They were long on tech jargon and short on marketing expertise. My first hurdle was to convince them they had to offer a money back guarantee after a one trial week. I had asked for a month trial, but they limited it to a week. I did not immediately pursue the tape issue, knowing that Frank would want me to drag the case out at least a few days, if not a few weeks. They gave me a demonstration machine and a list of prospective buyers who had responded to their ads. The buyers were mostly elderly and all in my familiar turf of West Los Angeles, West Hollywood, and Beverly Hills.

White noise is something that very few people can hear. The first elderly couple I demonstrated the machine for consisted of a wife named Ellen, who could not hear the white noise at all, and a husband named Marty, who thought he could hear it. Marty wanted the machine because Ellen was having trouble sleeping. Ellen complained, "Marty, I keep telling you the only reason I can't sleep is because of your snoring. Why spend money on a machine I can't even hear, when all we need is for you to wear that chin strap the doctor gave you to keep your mouth shut and stop you from snoring so loud?"

Marty obviously loved his wife. "But, Sweetheart, I can hear it. Mayb it'll work for you."

Ellen shook her head. "Marty, I think you're just hearing your tinnitus."

Marty pointed to me. " Young man, turn up the volume on that machine." I turned up the volume. Marty smiled eagerly at his wife. "There! Ellen, can you hear it now?"

Ellen stepped beside me and touched the volume control. "Let me see, maybe if I turned the volume up more. There, Marty, is it louder for you, too?"

Marty nodded and smiled. "Yes! Yes! It's louder now."

Ellen looked at him sadly. "Marty, I just turned the machine off. You're hearing your tinnitus. Please try wearing the chin strap tonight." She looked at me disdainfully. "I'm sorry we wasted your time, young man."

After three no-sales because I was trying to sell something they couldn't even hear, my second hurdle was to convince the company to add a sound effects 'loop' tape with a four track playback head and a switch that offered the options: midnight jungle, quiet forest, windy desert, and my favorite, sleepy lagoon, all sound effects tracks used in film editing. They still wanted to include the fifth option, white noise. I even designed a prototype of the loop player which was a miniaturized version of sound effects looping machines used in film editing. I showed them how they could build the loop player from stock parts in their store. They were resistant of the cost, but, when none of their few salesmen could sell even one machine, they made the revision and increased the price.

In the meantime, talking to store employees, I discovered the 3M tape in question was an archive from a defunct radio station which had recorded brand new tape only once before archiving it. I managed to get a copy of the check paid to the radio station by wooing a secretary. Frank sent the copy of the check and another sample tape from the archive being sold to 3M. In the time it took for their reply, the store made the modifications and I got to pitch the new machine to one final potential buyer.

This man lived N Hollywood near me and had risen from being a carpenter building film sets to being a top set designer. The walls of his home were adorned with his framed drawings of sets used in movies I had seen from the thirties and forties. When I demonstrated the machine, he recognized the sound effects tracks and asked me about the machines's construction. When I told him about my suggested modifications, he asked me, "Do you know who Les Paul and Mary Ford are?"

I nodded. "I know they're a performing duo who pioneered multi-track recording."

He smiled. "In 1955, Ross Snyder at Ampex built the first Sel-Sync 8-track machine which used one-inch tape. He sold it to Les Paul for ten thousand dollars, and that was the beginning of multi-track recording." He patted the machine. "What you've got here, its miniaturization and application, may be a sufficiently varied application of the multi-track system to warrant a patent. Have you tried to patent it?"

I rolled my eyes. "No. I'm just a salesman for the company that makes these."

He looked at me intently. "But it was your idea. You made the initial drawings."

I nodded. "Yes."

He looked at me eagerly. "Did you sign an employment contract with them?"

I inhaled deeply. "Yes."

His smile faded. "You're screwed. You work for them, any invention or intellectual property you create involving their product belongs to them." He shook his head. "Been there, suffered that. All the tools and techniques I developed belong to the studios I worked for. The money I spent on patent lawyers was wasted. And I know a dozen other friends whose inventions have made fortunes for their employers, and all they got was a pitiful mid-management annual salary." He patted the machine and smiled. "But, if not a bitter lesson learned, at least you made a sale today. If 'sleepy lagoon' doesn't put me to sleep, at least I can point to it and tell others about your clever application of a four track playback head."

When 3M closed the case with Frank and I told the store I was leaving, they begged me to stay, head their commission sales department, and utilize my down time as a floor salesman. I declined in favor of being free to pursue my film ambitions.

THE END

THE SMILE DOCTOR

In Hollywood there was a private hospital that catered to the most affluent citizens and provided the very best services in Hollywood's most needed specialities; i.e., plastic surgery, alcohol/drug rehabilitation, and obstetrics. The obstetrics included what was not called, but acted as, an abortion clinic, and the plastic surgery department included dentists, one of whom specialized in caps and called himself The Smile Doctor. The Smile Doctor was rich, handsome, and drove one of the first Corvettes to hit the market. He was a ladies man, and his wife wanted evidence of his infidelity to use as leverage in divorce court.

Although my forte as an investigator was audio recording and photography, two basic tools of a P.I are a gun and a car. My gun was a French MAB .380 caliber hammerless automatic pistol which I acquired as soon as I left the service. Having been shot at for a year in Korea, I felt insecure without the Colt .45 caber automatic pistol the Air Force had provided through most of my four years of military service. I had chosen the MAB because, being hammerless, it did not have a protruding hammer to get caught in my coat lining when carried in a shoulder holster, and, being a .380 calibre, it was smaller and lighter than a Colt .45. The MAB served my needs perfectly when I began to work as a private investigator. Fortunately, I never had to fire it, although I occasionally had to make it visible to de-escalate some situations. My car, however, was something else.

I was a great admirer of Dr Porche's Volkswagen and all its evolutions. In my lifetime I've owned twelve

Volskwagens; a bug sedan, a bug convertible, three ransporter vans, a Westphalia poptop camper van, five Karmen Ghia sedans, and one Karmen Ghia convertible. When I worked for Mark Angel, I owned a Karmen Ghia sedan. It looked great, handled well, and got great gas milage, but it was no Corvette.

Mark Angel had three investigators; John who owned a Dodge pickup truck equipped with a variety of guns, Tracey who owned a souped up Chevy sedan equipped with one of the first radio phones, and me with my Karmen Ghia equipped with a variety of still and movie cameras and tape recorders and mikes. Surveiling Doctor Smile was an assignment that should have gone to Tracey, but he was working for a client who required most of his duties be performed in her bedroom, and Mark was willing to pimp him out for as long as she paid his fees. I tried to refuse the Dr. Smile assignment, but Mark said he'd give me an extra dollar an hour to cover my gasoline expenses, and pay for all my food in the hospital cafeteria. At that time, I was collecting my Korean Veteran's unemployment compensation of twenty-five dollars a week, and desperate enough to accept six dollars an hour for an impossible assignment.

The one upside of the assignment was having to wait at the hospital until Dr. Smile left his office. The hospital kitchen provided gourmet food for the patient's rooms and the cafeteria. I ate very well after I convinced the cafeteria management that I was a bodyguard working for one of the patients, which became believable after they got the tiniest glimpse of the pistol in my shoulder holster and Mark Angel's office paid my tab. Flirting with Dr. Smile's receptionist and hinting that I could find her a bit part in the next movie I worked on won me her promise to call me on the pay phone in the cafeteria whenever he left.

55

The week or more I spent in that cafeteria, I saw almost as many celebrities as I did when I worked as a photographer and gossip writer for a publicist handling leading Hollywood restaurants. The food in the cafeteria was as good as some of those top flight restaurants, but I didn't have to write gossip about my fellow restaurant guests, although it was easy to tell who was there to dry out from alcohol or have an abortion or have a facelift, bust lift, or ass lift. It is weird to see a famously beautiful face turn purple during a nose job or without any teeth while acquiring new dentures.

The big downside of the assignment was that the Doctor drove his Corvette like the Freeway was a racetrack, and I could never keep up with him. I overtook him only twice when he got speeding tickets, but the tickets never slowed him down. As much as Mark angel wanted to stretch the assignment to increase his profits, he was getting desperate for some kind of progress to report to the wife. He began to hint that I should make up something to report like saying Dr. Smile stopped someplace and flirted with a waitress, or was seen picking up some woman who may or may not look like his dental assistant. Whenever I refused, he'd threaten to fire me if I didn't buy a more appropriate car.

The breakthrough came when the wife, who I had never met, visited Dr. Smile's office on some innocent wifely errand. The receptionist asked her if she had hired me, and the wife came to the cafeteria and introduced herself to me. When I confessed my race car problem in tailing her husband, she offered me a first name and phone number that she suspected was his mistress, having eavesdropped on his calls from their home and cleverly counting the clicks on the rotary dial phone used in those days. Without telling Mark and with that information, I located and staked out the suspected mistress's home, and, sure enough, Dr. Smile showed up regularly. Fortunately it was Summer and there was enough light at the time he arrived to get available light still photos with a telephoto lens of him kissing and groping the lady.

When I made an honest report of what happened, Mark was furious with me for not reporting my contact with the wife and for my initiative in reverse engineering the surveillance. I think he feared I would discover that he was charging clients a minimum of twenty-five dollars and hour plus padded expenses, and sometimes richer clients much more. I know he paid John much more tha Tracey or me, but John did some of the dirty work that Tracey and I wouldn't.

Dr. Smile's wife was a very attractive lady around fifty with a classic history of having helped put her husband through college, raised their children largely alone, and suffered his infidelity throughout their marriage. She was very polished and very much a lady, and not the first of Mark's female clients who made it obvious that the door was open to me. Because of her class and what might have been, I sometimes regretted not going through that door.

THE END

THE PRICE OF VANITY

Usually John Madden, Mark Angel's 'bad boy,' was hired out as a bodyguard, in part because he looked menacing with his long legs, pot belly, and pugnacious face with a spoonful of thin red hair on top. In other part because he delighted in using his fists and, I suspect, had used his gun on some occasions that were not always reported to the authorities. In the interest of the client's privacy, a lot of guidelines required in a private investigator's license were not necessarily followed or events reported to authorities.

I was assigned as a bodyguard to the family of a Beverly Hill's film producer for three reasons. One, because John Madden was on another assignment, two because I had better manners than John, and three because Mark regarded this client as a requiring a low level of security. He determined this when the wife's phone call included the explanation that, "My neighbor seems to think that she's so important she needs the protection of a bodyguard, and if she needs one, I certainly deserve one." When Mark offered her a uniformed security guard for less money instead, her reaction was, "If my neighbor has a plainclothes BODYGUARD, then I want a plainclothes BODYGUARD."

The first item on arrival was to identify all residents and staff of the household. The producer wasn't home, but pictures of him identified him as a fitiesh bald paunchy man with expensive tailoring and an excessive smile. The lady of the house had once been a beautiful blonde aspiring starlet who, after her film career plateaued, settled for being the trophy wife of a successful film producer The

58

skinny pimply faced sixteen year old son and the chubby bespectacled fifteen year old daughter had unfortunately inherited the worst genes of both parents. The maternal grandmother was once an 'A' list star whose career peaked after 'talkies' began in the thirties and her distinctive throaty voice was as sexy as her classic profile and trim figure. The staff consisted of a stout middle aged Mexican lady who was an efficient housekeeper, and a stout middle aged Hungarian houseman who was willing to wear a butler or a chauffeur's uniform whenever called for.

The next item was to inspect the house and grounds, install temporary battery operated alarms on all vulnerable doors and windows but the main front and back doors, and accept the wife's dictum that I couldn't put signs on the alarms that read, "Do Not Unlock, Do Not Open, Do Not Disarm."

The final item was to determine the location of my command post, the library off the main entrance hall, which gave me window surveillance of the front grounds, visibility of the entrance hall, and easy access to the front downstairs bathroom beneath and behind the curved staircase leading to the second floor. The rear downstairs bathroom was off the kitchen and usually reserved for the servants, but I had been given a dispensation to use the closer one under the stairs.

During the first of my twelve hour nightly shifts, the wife invited the neighbor lady over on some pretext so that she could answer the inevitable question, "Who is that strange man in the library?"

The wife resisted the temptation to gloat. "Oh, Max is my bodyguard. With the rise in crime, Julian doesn't want me to be unprotected at night. We suspect that I might have attracted some stalkers who recognized me from my old movies and followed me home." I nodded politely as the two women stared at me as if I were a newly acquired piece of furniture, barely nodding their heads in response.

The third night I was there, the grandmother came down the stairs in a tight fitting silver gown that showed her figure was as alluring as it had been in her early movies. The wife saw her headed for the library and followed her. As the grandmother approached me, her eyes lit up with recognition, and she spoke dramatically. "Oh, Stefan, my love! You've finally come home." She threw her arms around me and laid her head on my chest.

The wife looked at me apologetically. "I'm sorry, but my mother...."

The grandmother released me and looked at her daughter. "Lilly, go and get Stefan and me some tea."

The wife looked anxious. "Mother, it's me, Vera, your daughter."

The grandmother looked at Vera sternly. "Don't play games with me, Lilly. Go and get the tea."

Seeing Vera about to panic, I said, "Actually, M'am, I could use some coffee, if you don't mind."

The grandmother smiled at me. "Yes, of course, you prefer coffee." She looked condescendingly at Vera. "Go and get us coffee, Lilly, and use the good silver service." She looked at me lovingly. "After all, Stefan has finally come home to me." She gestured to the two seats separated by a coffee table by the window, and sat in one, looking at Vera sternly again. "Lilly, what are you waiting for? Go get the coffee, you silly girl!"

I nodded to the wife to indicate I was okay with the situation, and sat in the other chair as she went to order the coffee. The grandmother looked at me adoringly until her daughter was out of sight and hearing, then closed her eyes briefly as she laughed softly. "Oh, forgive me, young man. I know you're just Vera's latest trendy acquisition. As if

60

she needs a bodyguard. What she really needs is a body trainer. If she gets any more zoftic, my son-in-law will start banging his secretary, if he hasn't already."

I smiled. "I am impressed with your acting skills, young lady."

She smiled warmly at me. "Oh, I like you. I think you can understand why I like to make them think I have dementia. It's because they treated me like that for years. They even tried to have me committed so they could grab what's left of my money. Boy, were they shocked when I appeared lucid and bitched 'em out at the lawyer's office."

I laughed. "I would have loved to have seen that."

She shook her head. "Vera doesn't even recognize that my opening lines to you tonight were from one of my movies." She leaned back and her face softened into a compassionate expression. "The poor girl. Despite my agent's efforts, she never had a leading role. She thought that sleeping with producers would get her more than a few walk-ons or the opportunity to show off her body lounging at the pool in the background."

The housekeeper approached with a silver tray holding the silver coffee service, steam coming out of the spout of the silver coffee pot. She set the tray on the coffee table and whispered loudly to the grandmother. "Miss Sylvia, now you be nice to Miss Vera. I done wan her crying in my kitchen no more."

Sylvia shook her head. "Oh Maria, you know who is the real victim here."

Maria looked at me, then back at Sylvia and spoke in a disapproving tone. "El es un chico (He is a boy!). Tienes edad suficiente para ser su abuela. (You are old enough to be his grandmother.)."

Sylvia looked at me seductively. "El amor no tiene edad (Love has no age.)."

61

Maria turned her head to hear Vera's footsteps in he hall, then looked at Sylvia and hissed. "El amor no es lo mismo que la lujuria (Love is not the same as lust!)."

Vera approached. "I've told you two, only English in this house." Vera watched Maria exit, then looked at her mother angrily. "Mother, it's not fair to conspire with my housekeeper against me."

Sylvia adopted her movie role persona again. "Oh Lilly, to think you're still having P.M.S. at your age, and in front of Stefan, of all people!"

Vera clenched both fists at her sides in frustration, inhaled and exhaled deeply, then turned and left.

Sylvia poured our coffee, looked at me for approval of cream and sugar, and handed me my cup. "Don't judge me too harshly. Time has deprived me of several husbands and all the lovers I cared about. Even my agent is dead. If I let them, my daughter and her family will convince me that life is no longer worth living. The only things that keep me going are these little charades." She paused and looked at me seductively again as she sipped her coffee, "and an occasional man who finds his way to my room, the fifth door on the left at the top of the stairs. The one with my name engraved on a brass star from my old studio dressing room."

I ignored the invitation. "Why don't you resume your career. Surely there are plenty of mature roles out there."

She shook her head. "They'd rather put makeup on a younger actress willing to play an older roll." She sipped her coffee, sighed, and stared out the window. "Even though I never had to in the past, at this point I'd be willing to sleep with the bastard to get the role, but they'd rather sleep with the younger actress before she puts on the old lady makeup."

I shook my head. "They probably can't envision you in a mature role when you have the body of a nineteen year old."

She set her empty coffee cup on the tray and smiled at me. "Aren't you sweet." Then she rose, took three steps toward the hall, then turned and looked at me seductively again. "Remember, fifth door on the left at the top of the stairs. It's been unlocked ever since you arrived." Then she exited and I leaned forward to observe her ascending the stairs.

On my sixth night, I arrived to find a party planner and a catering staff frustrating the housekeeper and houseman with party preparations. I approached my post in the library, only to hear the two teenagers whispering angrily to each other. The boy hugged a brown paper bag to his chest with the necks of two bottles protruding from the top. "You tell mom about this and I'll tell her about you in that kitchen bathroom."

She wrinkled her nose beneath her black rimmed glasses. "You say anything about that and I'll not only tell her you stole two bottles of Scotch from the caterer, but also about the pot hidden in your closet. Besides, you don't know nothing about what goes on in there."

He laughed. "It's not too hard to guess when you and one of those old men come out of there fully dressed and he's zipping his fly while you're wiping jizz off your lips."

Her face began to flush. "Those 'old men,' as you call them, are 'A' list movie stars. You and your pimply face will never have sex with a movie star, or possibly never have sex with a woman."

He sneered at her. "I'd hardly call what you do having sex. They obviously don't want to stick their dicks in your pudgy body, and only about ten percent of them, the ones old enough to be your grandfather, are willing to stick their dicks in your pudgy four eyed face."

She sneered back at him. "You're just jealous because mom finds me more presentable to appear in public with her than you and all your tattoos and snotty attitude."

He nodded his head. "Oh yeah, how does she introduce you, 'this is my daughter who entertains at my parties by trapping old men in the kitchen bathroom and giving them blowjobs.'"

The girl raised both fists to strike him, but he grabbed both her wrists in his hands, dropping both bottles which crashed to the floor noisily. They both looked to the hall to see if anyone heard the crash, and saw me standing there. I moved forward immediately, as if I had just arrived. "Hello. You guys don't mind if I sit here by the window so I can watch the grounds and the hallway, do you?"

The girl looked panicked and mumbled, "How long you been there?"

I acted innocent. "Where? I just came through the front door. Did I miss something?"

We all looked at the pool of Scotch, broken glass, and torn bag on the floor. The boy stammered, "I'll go get Maria to clean this up."

The girl looked confused. "Yeah, I'll go get...I'll...I'll just go," and she exited hastily.

If this family really needed security, they would have needed at least six bodyguards for a party, but, in reality, the aged guests were extremely safe and civil, give or take some of the men who frequented the kitchen bathroom. The age group in attendance reflected the fact that Sylvia, not Vera the hostess, was the primary attraction, and the producer's few star guests were comparable 'B' listers.

Toward the end of the evening, Sylvia stood before me, smiling at me as I sat in my chair. "You know you don't have to sit here so diligently. You could circulate, if you like. Nobody here will become unruly and have to be bounced out on their ear, and none of my daughter's imagined stalkers are going to abduct her and carry her off into the night, although there are moments I wish they would."

I pointed to a generous plate of canapes and a coffee Maria had provided me on the coffee table. "I'm fine. I have everything I need."

Sylvia stepped closer until our knees almost touched. She leaned down and picked a shrimp off my plate, then stood up and stared at me as she put it in her mouth, pinched the tail, and slowly suctioned the pink body between her ruby red lips until it disappeared. Then she set the tail shell on my plate, smiled, and said, "Well, if you need anything else....anything....the fifth door on the left is still unlocked," then she slowly exited. Once again, I leaned forward to watch her ascend the stairs.

The most tragic and revealing member of this household was not human. The neighbor lady had acquired a tiny Yorkshire terrier puppy with a cute face and large pointed ears. She brought the dog over in an oversized teacup to emphasize how miniature it was. Her excuse for showing off her acquisition was to announce that, because the dog was small enough to escape any opening in the yard fence, her neighbors should know who it belonged to and return it if it appeared in their yard. Of course, the exorbitant price the animal cost managed to slip into the conversation.

Vera got the message that a cute and expensive pet was as much a status symbol as an expensive car or a bodyguard, particularly if it was small enough to fit in your purse and be a conversation piece at luncheons. As soon as the neighbor lady left, Vera was on the phone to the nearest pet shop.

By the time my next shift began, a messenger had arrived with a pink cardboard animal carrier shaped like a ladies hat box. Out came an adorable Yorkshire terrier with a wagging tale, an eternal smile, and a compulsion to greet everyone and attempt to lick their face. He immediately won the women's hearts, and even inspired smiles on the faces of the teenage son and the houseman. Vera named him Truffles, after her favorite and most expensive chocolate candy, and he was given an elaborate velvet bed in the kitchen with golden colored food and water bowls and his framed pedigree papers on the wall behind it.

But, as Vera held the adorable puppy in front of her just far enough to foil his attempts to kiss her face, her smile slowly faded. She commented that he was not quite as tiny as her neighbor's dog, although that may have been the difference of a week or so in their ages. Then she noticed that his ears were not quite as large and would sometimes flop over instead of standing straight up. Maria suggested that they may firm up as he grew, and to give it a week or more to do so.

After scrutinizing the status of his ears for five days, Vera decided to send him to the vet. The vet sent him back with cardboard cones on his ears, which Truffles promptly removed. After a second visit to the vet, who informed Vera that his ears could not be corrected surgically, Truffles came back with ear cones and a collar around his neck to prevent him from removing the cones. Each time he returned, Truffles looked sadder and ever so slightly less sociable. Each time Vera inspected his ears with a judgmental expression, the poor little puppy would whimper and try harder to kiss her, and look so sad when she'd set him down without smiling or letting him kiss her. Finally, he took to hiding in the cabinet under the sink, and slunk away from anyone's effort to pet or hold him.

When the shop refused to take Truffles back, Vera found another dealer and bought an even smaller Yorkshire terrier than her neighbors. The daughter insisted on naming the new dog Snickers, after the daughter's favorite candy bar. Snickers ears were huge and pointy and stiff, which noticeably pleased Vera. However, Snickers was not affectionate, didn't smile or kiss or wag his tail much, and was aloof with most people. The only person he'd let pick him up was Vera. Sylvia said he was the reincarnation of her cold, insensitive, impotent third husband.

After Snicker's arrival, the only people who tried to communicate with Truffles were Sylvia, Maria, and myself. Even then you would have to coax him out from under the sink and he would tremble if you pet him and pee nervously if you tried to pick him up, which made the rest of the family shun him more. When Vera said it would be kinder to put him to sleep, Maria asked her to let Maria take Truffles home to her grandchildren, which she did. Later, when I asked Maria how Truffles was doing, she looked sad and said, "Bedder, but he still spooked if you try to pet or hold him. Bud he no live under de sink no more."

Several days after Truffles left, I went to the front downstairs bathroom and, through the open door, saw the daughter looking in the mirror, pulling her hair back to inspect her ears, pulling the skin under her chin to measure her fat, and pulling the skin to the side of her cheeks to reduce her jowls. She turned her head to the left, then the right, then held her hands on either side of her face to see what it would look like if it were less round.

67

On several occasions I noticed the son develop a nervous facial tick, a clenching of one side of his mouth, each time any mention was made of his appearance, or any question was asked about his future employment. Maria learned that she should never mention Truffles name in Vera's presence. When a seam in the husband's pants burst, Sylvia quipped he better lose weight "or Vera may have you put to sleep and replaced with a smaller model."

That remark almost brought tears to Vera's eyes and prompted the equally bitter retort of, "Perhaps you should keep your sarcasms to yourself, or you may have to see how much they're appreciated by fellow residents in a nursing home."

I don't think that wealth creates a dysfunctional family, although it may exaggerate the dysfunction. Rather it is vanity, the lust for image and the compulsion to compete, that diminishes, distracts, or destroys a parent's instinct to nurture and support. I spent six weeks in that household before the husband decided that Mark Angel's price exceeded any benefits to his wife's vanity. But I think a greater price was paid by all members of that family, none more than Truffles.

THE END

PRIDE AND PREJUDICE

As I approached the Brown Derby Restaurant on Vine Street in Hollywood, I thought to myself that it should be called the Mission Restaurant because of its red tiled roof with vegas sticking out of the roof eaves and its arched main door, much like a Southwest Spanish Mission. It certainly didn't look like the original Brown Derby Restaurant on Wilshire Boulevard in a building which was actually shaped like a brown derby hat. But the Brown Derby Restaurant on Vine Street in Hollywood was probably more famous because it was the site of so many major Hollywood deals and dramas. It had been founded by Herbert Somborn, one of Gloria Swanson's husbands. Clerk Gable had proposed to Carole Lombard there. Columnists Louella Parsons and Hedda Hopper trolled the place frequently looking for juicy gossip.

Louella and Hedda would have probably liked to know why I was lunching there with Mark Angel's new client, a famous film director whom my publisher's lawyers say I should refer to as Mr. John Smith. When I approached Mr. Smith at one of the less conspicuous rear tables, I noticed his hair was a lot grayer than when I watched him walk up to the Oscar's podium years before on T.V.. As I extended my hand in introduction and began to sit, he looked around the room cautiously before shaking my hand. He spoke in almost a whisper. "Does anybody here know who you are.....I mean, what you are?"

I thought to myself that I shouldn't take offense to the question or my answer, because it was a question I often asked myself when working for Mark Angel's clients. "No sir. I am no one and nothing to anyone who might see us together."

He looked relieved as he sat back in his chair after half rising to shake my hand. "Good! I mean....no offense to you or your profession. It's just that I didn't want to be seen going into Mr. Angel's office a second time, and, well.....you know."

I smiled reassuringly. "No problem, sir. You may count on our discretion. I have signed a confidentiality agreement with Mr. Angel's office regarding all my work for all his clients. In your case, I happen to also be a photographer and a cinematographer, and, if it makes you feel more comfortable, you may refer to me as such to anyone who approaches us or sees us together."

His bushy eyebrows raised. "Oh really! Have you done any feature work, anything I might have seen?"

I shrugged. "Perhaps a few fleeting seconds of an establishing shot like a New Orleans Mardi Gras in full swing or a Jamaican sunset over the twin harbors of Port Antonio, or perhaps a few trick shots like a car going over a cliff in Malibu canyon."

He nodded. "So you do pickup shots?"

I nodded. "Yes, but you'll never see my name in the credits because I'm not in the union."

He shook his head. "Yeah, I know. And you'll never see the basement price they paid you on the accounting sheets, because they listed a much larger amount in their nephew's name and pocketed the difference, right?"

I smiled. "Confidentiality prevents me from answering that question, sir."

He chuckled. "Okay, young man, you've won my confidence with the fact that you're a cinematographer, and that you're a Southerner."

I was surprised. "And what makes you think I'm a Southerner? Do you hear an accent?"

He shook his head. "No, no! In fact, I was surprised I didn't hear an accent. Mr. Angel told me you were a Southerner. You are, aren't you? I suspect that's where the footage of a New Orleans Mardi Gras comes from. Am I right?"

I sighed. "You are right, Sir, but I'm curious as to why being a Southerner matters."

The waiter arrived and Mr. Smith smiled when I declined the offer of an alcoholic beverage. I ordered a pastrami on rye with coffee, and he ordered a Cobb salad with Earl Grey tea. When the waiter left, Mr. Smith narrowed his eyes as he looked at me. "Mind you, I am not a racist or a bigot, and I don't assume you to be, but, being a Southerner, I'm hoping you'll tolerate my one bias that applies in this case."

I tilted my head. "And what bias might that be?"

He closed his eyes for three seconds, then looked at me. "I am a devout Catholic and I have never considered divorcing my wife, for whom I've provided a wonderful life of luxury. But I have also loved and lost other women, and I have always lost them to Latin lovers. Georgiana Belzer, Loretta Young's sister, ended up marrying the Mexican actor Ricardo Montalban. Arlene Dahl ended up marrying the Argentine actor Fernando Lamas. Lucille Ball ended up marrying the Cuban band leader Desi Arnaz. And Cecil B. deMille's daughter, Agnes deMille, ended up marrying another Mexican actor, Anthony Quinn. For an Irishman who only dated white girls, Latin lovers became my nemesis."

I looked at Mr. Smith's white hair and thought to myself, "I hope Mark Angel didn't expect me to be a hit man and get rid of the Latin lover of this old guy's latest girlfriend. If that's the case, he should've sent John Madden, who is also an Irishman." Instead of voicing my thought, I tried to keep a straight face and said, "While your romantic competitors may have shared a Hispanic heritage, they also shared your good taste in women and your appreciation of beauty. Am I to assume that yet another Latin lover has encroached upon your relationship with another lady in your life?"

He clenched his teeth before answering. "Yes and no. I'm a little over the hill as far as any romantic relationships. The lady in my life in this case is my grown daughter who was divorced several years ago. The Latin lover in this case is not a famous actor, at least not to my knowledge. Who and what he is is why I hired you. All I know about him is that he is Mexican, appears to be younger than my daughter, and smiles at me as we cross paths outside my daughter's door, giving me that 'you know I'm fucking your daughter' look. I saw that same smug look on all the others faces."

I felt relieved he didn't expect any strong arm stuff from me. "Did you try to discuss him with your daughter?"

He frowned. "Of course, but she wouldn't say anything about him other than that he was a friend. When I asked if he was her boyfriend, she said, 'Just a friend.' But I don't believe her. I know that smug expression on their faces all too well." He handed me a letter size kraft envelope. "Here's her recent photo, her address, her phone number in case you're able to tap it, and both my office and home phone numbers, but I assume you wont discuss anything regarding this affair with anyone that answers, other than me."

I took the envelope. "Actually, I wont be contacting you. Mark Angel will contact you with any information I procure, giving you periodic updates by phone, and a final detailed written report at the conclusion of the assignment."

His frown softened. "I kinda would like to hear it all from you in person. Sometimes things get lost in translation, and, besides, I believe in the personal touch. That's why I wanted to have lunch with the person who's actually gonna do the spying. Mr. Angel is impressive with his gung ho F.B.I. background and all, God, the man looks like Dick Tracy with white hair, but I'd like to hear the worst from someone a little more human." He reached in his coat pocket and pulled out an unmarked plain white number ten envelope, handing it to me. "You can still make all your proper reports to Mr. Angel, but take this, and promise me you'll update me personally by phone of anything significant, and that you'll have lunch with me again when this is all over. There'll be another envelope for you then."

I looked in the open envelope at five one hundred dollar bills, probably twice what I would earn from Mark Angel on this assignment. "You realize my boss is still gonna bill you his usual fees."

He shrugged and started to rise. "I understand, but Mr. Angel doesn't have to know anything about our arrangement, or the envelope I just gave you, or about our final lunch. Okay?"

I took my last sip of coffee, stood up, extended my hand with a smile, and said, "Okay."

****

In the late 1950's, despite the introduction of commercial broadcast television in the late 1940's, there was no consumer or security video equipment available.

Private investigators relied on still photos and 16mm motion picture footage for evidence, which is one of the reasons Mark Angel hired me. The other reason is that, because I had to understand and accommodate sound technicians during theatrical filming, I understood and could operate sound recording equipment.

My specialized investigator's arsenal consisted of 35mm single lens reflex still cameras and 16mm reflex movie cameras with long telephoto lenses that could spy from a distance, and small motorized 35mm cameras and 16mm 50' magazines cameras that could be concealed in books and briefcases for closeups. For audio, I hid a battery operated reel to reel recorder in a briefcase, and had a brick sized 'concealed' Mohawk Midgitape Recorder which, when slung in a holster inside my coat, made me look like I was packing a Colt 45 automatic pistol. Wireless microphones, necessary for remote recording, were rare and expensive items. I made extra money from Mark Angel by wiring single transistor microphone transmitters and encapsulating them in epoxy in a plastic ice cube tray. In the few years I worked for Mark Angle, I sold him the first dozen I made in a single ice cube tray for $50 apiece.

I introduced myself to Mr. Smith's daughter, Barbara, as a telephone serviceman, wearing my fatigues from my former military service which still had the light green outline of the two stripes I had removed from the sleeves, which she never noticed. My disguise included a false mustache and bushy eyebrows purchased in the children's toy department of a dimestore. I installed a wireless microphone in her phone and another in a centrally located electrical duplex outlet. Finding someplace to survey her apartment was much harder. I finally had to bribe a college student in an adjacent apartment house to let me set up my hidden cameras, tape recorder, and shotgun microphone in his living room which had a window with a view of her living room and bathroom windows,. Although the bathroom window was only partially open at the top, the mirror over the handbasin provided a view of the upper half of the room, including the top of the door which announced the entrance and exit of anyone in the room.

It took me only two days to take pictures of Ramon, her Mexican 'friend,' and record conversations that made it obvious he was not her lover, but, rather, her pusher. His visits never lasted longer than ten minutes, and were always followed by her solo visit to the bathroom. All I had to see was her raise the hypodermic needle in the air to expel any air bubbles from it, which verified the recorded references to 'horse' and haggling over price. Barbara was addicted to heroin, which may or may not have contributed to her divorce.

Another factor which may have contributed to her divorce was the fact that she did, indeed, have a lover. Mr. Smith might be pleased to know that his daughter's lover was not Latin, but, in fact, a rather well known Anglo-Saxon. While that might be the good news I could deliver, I suspected he would interpret the gender of his daughter's lover as bad news. His daughter's lover was an A-list actress who, from my recorded conversations, was growing weary of Barbara's heroin addiction.

My phone conversations with Mr. Smith and Mark Angel required the utmost tact. I knew Mark would not want to close the case after two days. He always wanted to milk every case for two weeks or as long as he could. So my queries to Mr. Smith (Was Barbara a diabetic or have a heart condition or use B12 shots?), had to be phrased so the truth was not too evident and his answers could help rule out any other assumptions regarding what I saw and heard. As with other cases, I decided I would let Mark push it unnecessarily beyond one week, but find some excuse to cut it short of two weeks. Saving the client a little bit at the end of the case would ease my conscience a little bit regarding the guilt I felt about most of the work I did for Mark. The irony was that Mark's greed paid off in an unexpected way. Something happened on the tenth night, the night I would have insisted to Mark we close the case.

That night the pusher had come and gone, and the lesbian lover had arrived to find Barbara nodding off from the heroin. The lover delivered an ultimatum, which Barbara reacted to by threatening suicide and locking herself in the bathroom. The lover didn't believe her, but I saw the hypodermic raised in the air for the second time within a few hours, and it looked pretty full to me. I raced from one apartment house to the other, arriving at Barbara's door as her lover was leaving. I raised both hands to stop her and spoke with urgency. "Do you have a key?"

She spoke with defiance and anger. "Who the hell are you?"

I waved my hands again to stop her. "I just saw Barbara shoot up for the second time in three hours, and I think she fell to the floor."

The lover looked undecided, but then began to retrieve her key from her purse and unlock the door. We both rushed to the bathroom door, which was locked, and the lover began banging on it repeatedly as she spoke. "Barbara, you crazy bitch, open this door! Barbara, I was just angry, I didn't mean it, Sweetie, open the door."

I gestured for her to move back. She frowned at me and asked, "What are you going to do? I pay the rent on this apartment and, if you break down that door, it's coming out of my security deposit!"

I looked at her incredulously. "Are you kidding?"

She closed her eyes and held her head in both hands. "I'm sorry! Go ahead."

I kicked in the door and kneeled beside Barbara who lay on the floor, her eyes closed and the hypodermic needle a foot from her arm. I checked her carotic artery and then her wrist. Her heart rate was already dangerously weak and slow. I put the needle in my pocket and picked Barbara up in my arms, saying to her lover. "I drive a Karmen Ghia. It's too small to put her in the back seat. What do you drive?"

It was obvious her lover had ambivalent feelings about the whole situation. "We'll put her in my Cadillac, but you've gotta go with her and take her into emergency. I can't go in. You understand?"

I nodded and followed her with Barbara in my arms as she locked the apartment door and led me down to her car. En route, I told her I was a P.I., but not who I worked for. The lover kept fishing for the name my client; Barbara's husband, Barbara's father, Barbara's possible other female or male lover. No mention was ever made of the lover's identity or celebrity, or Barbara's relationship to Hollywood nobility.

The Los Angeles County General Hospital was an imposing 1930's concrete edifice which everyone at that time identified as the title background for the daytime T.V. soap opera, *General Hospital.* It's emergency entrance was a curvy uphill driveway which the lover negotiated with squealing tires and an abrupt stop that almost crashed into a parked County ambulance. The instant I removed Barbara from the rear seat and, balancing her in my arms, kicked the rear door shut, the lover took off with burning rubber and squealing tires. Attendants rushed a Gurney to me and I placed Barbara on it. I followed them into Minor Trauma as a nurse walked beside me with a clipboard, and I handed her the needle, saying, "I think this is heroin."

Two hours later I found a phone booth in the hospital cafeteria, which only served coffee and doughnuts at that hour. I called Mr. Smith and we had the following conversation:

ME: "Mr. Smith, you said to call you with anything significant."

MR. SMITH: "Yes, but is it significant enough to call me at three in the morning?"

ME: I'll let you decide that, Sir. First, the good news is that the man you thought was your daughter's Latin lover is not her lover. He is a Puerto Rican named Ramon Escariz. The bad news is that he IS her pusher, and this evening she almost overdosed on heroin, but she's in stable condition at General Hospital where I brought her a couple hours ago."

MR. SMITH: "Oh no, not again. I spent a fortune drying her out. She was doing so good. I bet it was that damn Mexican lover who led her astray again."

ME: "Well, to quote you, Sir, yes and no. Yes, he was probably party to leading her astray, but, no, he's not Mexican and he's not her lover."

MR. SMITH: "Of course, of course. You just told me that. YOU took her to the hospital? Thank God it wasn't the police, but how did that come about, and what did you tell them?"

ME: "During surveillance I saw her overdosing, so I took her to the hospital and identified her as my sister using her first name and my last name. I said she was visiting me and I gave my address as her temporary address, and myself as first of kin."

MR. SMITH: "Oh, thank God! Good man! Good man! Are you still with her? What'll we do when she wakes up? I can't show my face there or I might be identified. You understand, don't you?"

ME: "Yes, Sir, I understand. I'll remain with her until she wakes, and I'll try to steer her clear of your name or her married name. If she sticks with my claim that she's a visitor, they probably wont invoke any police or rehab intervention. But she doesn't know who I am or why I would register her under my name. Do you want me to tell her who I am and why I was observing her, or do you want me to have her call you and let you explain?"

There was a long pause before he answered.

MR. SMITH: "Tell her to call me. And tell Mark Angel to close the case."

ME; "You'll have to tell him, Sir. I'm not supposed to contact you directly. Remember?"

MR. SMITH: "Yes, yes, of course. I'll call him tomorrow, or rather, in a few hours. But I want to have lunch with you in the next few days, and I'll have another envelope to give you then. Okay?"

Three days later he wanted to meet at Sharp's Cafeteria, a working man's eatery a half block from the Hollywood Post Office. He started apologizing as he set his tray down on the small bare formica table at te rear of the room. "I decided to avoid The Brown Derby. I doubt anyone here would ever know me. I hope this is okay with you."

I put sugar in my coffee. "Fine. I have a P.O. box at the post office, and I lunch here from time to time. How is your daughter?"

He smiled. "She's fine, thank you. She's back in her apartment. I wanted her to stay at my place, but she refused, so I hired a nurse to stay with her for a few days and extracted a promise from Barbara that she wouldn't let that Mexican....that Puerto Rican bastard near her place again." He pulled out a white number ten envelope and held it in front of his face. "I hope you find this sufficient for all you've done, but also sufficient enough to tell me everything that I should know."

I sighed. "Does that mean I can decide what you should know, or does that mean I should tell you absolutely everything?"

He frowned. "I would prefer ABSOLUTELY everything."

I bit my lip. "In that case, as much as it pains me to say it, perhaps you should keep that envelope."

His frown turned to a pained smile as he handed the envelope to me. "Okay. Have it your way. Now tell me what you think I should know."

I accepted the open envelope and peered inside at ten one hundred dollar bills. "Well, Sir, I suspect you know more about your daughter's addition to heroin than I do. Suffice it to say her pusher visits her daily and it's probably quality stuff because it's costing her a hundred dollars a day."

His eyes widened. "How can she afford that? She's not getting that much from me!"

I sipped my coffee. "I told you Mr. Escariz was not her lover, but she does have a lover, and maybe that accounts for part of her income."

He frowned. "Well he must be a wealthy son of a bitch, and he's probably a junkie, too, if he's willing to feed her habit."

I shook my head. "No sir, I have good reason to believe this person is not an addict, and equal reason to believe this person disapproved of your daughter's habit and made repeated efforts to stop her from using."

He looked angry. "Okay then, tell me who he is and I'll thank him for those efforts."

I sighed. "That, sir, is information I feel you should request of your daughter, not me."

He clenched his teeth. "I don't want to sound crass, but I'm paying you well for this information. I think I deserve to know a little more about him. What ethic would you be violating by telling me his name?"

I returned his stern glare. "The same ethic that made me protect your good name at the hospital." I softened my glare, then asked, "I'm not a psychiatrist, but would you care to hear my take on what may relate to your daughter's lover and your daughter's addiction?"

He nodded. "Of course, if he's the cause of her addiction, I want to know."

I winced. "I don't think her lover is the cause of her addiction, but rather her lover's gender. I think your daughter may see you as having a bias towards certain categories of people, and the stress of hiding the fact that she's gay from you may relate to her addiction."

Not only did his eyes widen, but his jaw dropped open. He stared at me in shock for almost thirty seconds as I busied myself with my corned beef sandwich. Then he took a deep breath and looked at the egg salad sandwich on his plate. "You're telling me that Barbara's fear of my being a bigot has destroyed her life."

I washed a bite of corned beef down with some coffee. "I prefer the term you used about yourself, probably all of us sometimes harbor a 'bias.' Have you ever expressed a bias toward gay people to your daughter?"

He closed his eyes and shook his head. "Oh God, yes, so many times. I trashed Rock Hudson and so many of those bastards who pretended to be God's gift to women, then went home at the end of the day and sodomized little boys on their silken sheets. I'm sure I was as vitriolic in my references to Marlene Dietrich and all the other hypocritical bull dykes I know in Hollywood." He looked at me with watery eyes. "What I thought of as family values must've been like a dagger in her heart."

I tried to sound sympathetic. "You are not solely to blame. You were simply reflecting society's majority attitude toward gay culture. And your daughters life is not destroyed, because her life is not over. There is life after addiction, and you have the option to tell her that your attitudes have changed, if that be the case."

It was obvious his moment of compassion for his daughter had changed as he stood up, leaving his sandwich and iced tea untouched. "It is obvious what your attitude is, but mine is unchanged. The good news is that I am fortunate that Mark Angel assigned you to me. I appreciate your resourcefulness and your tact in dealing with the situation. You actually saved her life, and I hope that envelope compensates you adequately for that. What you may regard as the bad news is that I know of a rehab facility which not only claims they can cure heroin addiction, but that they can also reprogram gays back into heterosexuals. It worked for an actor friend of mine on two of his sons, and I'm sending Barbara there whether she likes it or not."

I was in shock as he extended his hand to me and I slowly raised mine. He smiled as he shook my hand vigorously and said, "Enjoy your lunch," and left.

Two famous phrases came to my mind; the title of Jane Austin's 1813 novel, *Pride and Prejudice*, which, to me, personified Mr. Smith, and Oscar Wilde's line, "No good deed goes unpunished," which personified the mistake I had just made.

THE END

OTHER BOOKS BY WILLIAM KARL THOMAS

All books are available in print and digital E-editions from Amazon.com, or from any bookseller via the books ISBN number. Autographed copies are available from Media Maestro - Book Division, P.O. Box 50672, Tucson, AZ 85703, or online at www.mediamaestro.net.

THE RELUCTANT HOLLYWOOD P.I. The book you have just read is available in an E-edition for your Kindle, Nook, I-pad, or other E-reader, or read it on your computer by downloading Amazon's free E-reader application. Tell your friends they can buy the E-edition online for less than it would cost to mail your print copy.

ISBN #978-0-9799477-3-5 Softcover: $9.95
ISBN #978-0-9799477-7-3 Digital E-edition $2.99

HOLLYWOOD TALES FROM THE OUTER FRINGE

Thomas' career brought him in contact with 'A' list celebrities and the armies of 'little people' who served them. This anthology of 12 stories reveals the intimate relationship between the two set against a historically accurate 1950's-1960's background. Love Hollywood's down and dirty side, then you've gotta love the torrid twisted "Hollywood Tales From The Outer Fringe."

ISBN #978-0-9799477-3-5 Softcover: $9.95
ISBN #978-0-9799477-7-3 Digital edition: $2.99

LENNY BRUCE: THE MAKING OF A PROPHET

Thomas' intimate and poignant memoir of his ten year collaboration with the most controversial comedian of the 20th century, a martyr to First Amendment rights. The book begins before Bruce's rise to international fame and continues through the night Bruce died.

ISBN #978-0-9799477-0-4 Hardcover $24.95
ISBN #978-1-62768-003-5 Softcover $9.95
ISBN #978-0-9799477-4-2 Digital E-edition $4.99

THE CANDY BUTCHER

The amazing biography of screenwriter, film producer, playwright, actor, nightclub comedian Frank Ray Perilli, creator of such notable films as *The Doberman Gang, Harlow* and such cult films as *Dracula's Dog, Little Cigars, Fairytales, Cinderella, The End of the World, Alligator,* and more than two dozen unique offbeat films and plays.

ISBN 978-1-62768-019-6 Softcover $9.95
ISBN:978-1-62768-020-2 Digital E-edition $2.99

THE PIANO LOVER a trilogy
In New Orleans French Quarter during the 1950's, a young male cocktail pianist's life is complicated by four beautiful women: two young women from opposite poles of society who love him in diverse ways, and two middle aged women who seek to control him for their own secret reasons.

ISBN #978-1-62768-005-9 Softcover $14.95
ISBN: 978-1-62768-006-6 digital E-edition $4.99

PIANO LOVER: THE MUSICAL
The second novel of *The Piano Lover* trilogy includes the script and score of an entire original musical stage production. Follow the careers of the talented alumni from New Orleans French Quarter who helped create the 1950's and 1960's counter culture.

ISBN #978-1-62768-011-0 Softcover $14.95
ISBN: 978-1-62768-012-7 digital E-edition $4.99

PIANO LOVER: THE MOVIE
In the third novel of the trilogy, the musical is made into a movie. The entourage experience professional and romantic adventures in Hollywood, San Francisco, and exotic foreign capitals with their famous and celebrated show biz peers.

ISBN #978-1-62768-013-4 Softcover $14.95
ISBN: 978-1-62768-014-1 digital E-edition $4.99

CLEO
A novel about a beautiful and talented black female journalist who is an intimate friend of black entertainment and political celebrities during the turbulent civil rights era in the 1950's and 1960's. Her professional and private life takes a quantum leap when she crosses paths with a cynical but equally talented white male publicist.

ISBN: 978-1-62768-002-8 Softcover $9.95
ISBN: 978-0-9799477-6-6 digital E-edition $2.99

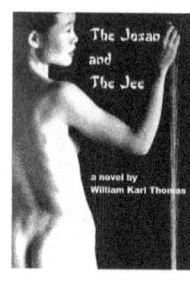

THE JOSAN AND THE JEE
A novel about three women who survived massacres and rape during The Korean War, and their intimate relationship with an American GI dealing with his own demons from his failed marriage to his unfaithful stateside wife to his contentious relationship with his bigoted military boss.

ISBN: 978-1-62768-001-1 Softcover $9.95
ISBN: 978-0-9799477-5-9 digital E-edition $2.99
I   `

THE GENTEEL POOR

A memoir telling the story of four generations of the author's colorful and talented family spanning the Civil War, World War I, the Great Depression, and World War II. This coming of age memoir deals with the social and ethnic evolution of the New Orleans/Gulf Coast area a century before it was devastated by Hurricane Katrina.

ISBN: 978-1-59663-565-4 Hardcover: $29.95
ISBN: 978-1-62768-000-4 Softcover $9.95
ISBN: 978-0-9799477-9-7 digital E-edition $2.99

A PLACE FOR US

The biography of Wendy Wolf who entered an iron lung at the age of four and emerged a polio survivor whose life illustrates the challenges of opportunity and acceptance people with disabilities face and the triumphs and successes this extraordinary woman achieved.

ISBN: 978-0-9799477-2-8 Hardcover $29.95
ISBN: 978-1-62768-004-2 Softcover $9.95
ISBN: 978-0-9799477-8-0 digital E-edition $2.99

IMMORTAL: a science fiction trilogy
A millennium into the future, three alien archeologists attempt to determine how humanity self destructed themselves and their planet. Their discovery of a dormant android guarding a human gene bank on a Saturnian moon leads to a conflict among them regarding humanity's potential future. Share the alien archeologist's discovery of human evolution and the turning points that shaped earth's civilizations in the first book of this trilogy.
ISBN: 978-1-62768-007-3 Softcover $9.95
ISBN: 978-1-62768-008-0 digital E-edition $2.99

IMMORTAL: RESURRECTION
In the second novel of the trilogy, the alien females' experience as a galactic explorer is revealed. She allies herself with the android's desperate attempt to resurrect humanity while alien forces mount an expedition to rid the universe of human dysfunctional behavior.
ISBN: 978-1-62768-015-8 Softcover $9.95
ISBN: 978-1-62768-016-5 digital E-edition $2.99

IMMORTAL: ARMAGEDDON
In the third novel of the trilogy, a small band of newly created humans defend the survival of the human race against an alien expedition determined to rid the universe of future human folly, and the origin and mission of the android is revealed.
ISBN: 978-1-62768-017-2 Softcover $9.95
ISBN: 978-1-62768-018-9 digital E-edition $2.99

ABOUT THE AUTHOR

 William Karl Thomas was born 1/25/33 in Bay St. Louis, Mississippi, a small Gulf Coast town in which Tennessee Williams lived and wrote about in his works. In 1951 Thomas married his former high school teacher and was divorced after a four year childless marriage. His checkered background includes being a cocktail pianist in New Orleans French Quarter, serving a year of combat in the Air Force as a military correspondent during the Korean War, being a photographer, a journalist, a feature/documentary cinematographer, a screen writer, an industrial film producer, a public relations executive, and a book author. He has worked for and with such notables as Frank Sinatra, the Rat Pack, Lenny Bruce, and others..
In the course of various assignments, Thomas has lived or worked in Oxford England, Paris France, Japan, Korea, Jamaica, Mexico, Canada, and various parts of the United States.

The Manchester Guardian has stated, "He superbly evokes the seedy atmosphere of the cheap Hollywood clubs and coffeehouses," and "His work sometimes reads like a Bogart script." Kirkus refers to, "His historically astute depiction of the country and era" and "(He) aptly conveys the heights and depths of human capability," and refers to *The Josan and the Jee* as "An emotionally challenging but rewarding war novel." Readers reviews say " One of the best books I have ever read; maybe the best," and "This story will make you sad and happy at the same time. It is difficult to put the book down."

www.ingramcontent.com/pod-product-compliance
Lightning Source LLC
Chambersburg PA
CBHW071632140626
46555CB00022B/2624